Sadie closed her ey[es]
brush of Michael's lips on hers.

It was wonderful. Exhilarating. Exactly the way homecoming is supposed to feel.

Madness.

She pulled away from him. "That didn't help."

"My morning feels helped quite a lot."

"It didn't help how mixed-up I feel!"

"I don't intend to help you with that." He grinned at her as he walked out the back door. She watched him cross the yard, saw him pause to throw a ball to Tucker and drop on his knee to speak to Amber.

She could yell at him to never come back. But he might listen. Like last time.

And for a moment, everything she had ever wanted in the whole world seemed to be hers. A breathtakingly handsome man, children playing in the sunshine.

An illusion, she told herself. The kids weren't hers.

And Michael most certainly wasn't hers.

Dear Reader,

Welcome to another wonderful month at Silhouette Romance. In the midst of these hot summer days, why not treat yourself (come on, you know you deserve it) by relaxing in the shade with these romantically satisfying love stories.

What's a millionaire bachelor posing as a working-class guy to do after he agrees to baby-sit his cranky infant niece? Run straight into the arms of a very beautiful pediatrician who desperately wants a family of her own, of course! Don't miss this delightful addition to our BUNDLES OF JOY series with *Baby Business* by Laura Anthony.

The ever-enchanting award-winning author Sandra Steffen is back with the second installment of her enthralling BACHELOR GULCH miniseries. This time it's the local sheriff who's got to lasso his lady love in *Wyatt's Most Wanted Wife*.

And there are plenty of more great romances to be found this month. Moyra Tarling brings you an emotionally compelling marriage-of-convenience story with *Marry In Haste*. A gal from the wrong side of the tracks is reunited with the sexy fire fighter she'd once won at a bachelor auction (imagine the interesting stories they'll have to tell) in Cara Colter's *Husband In Red*. RITA Award-winning author Elizabeth Sites is back with a terrific Western love story centering around a legendary wedding gown in *The Rainbow Bride*. And when best friends marry for the sake of a child, they find out that real love can follow, in *Marriage Is Just the Beginning* by Betty Jane Sanders.

So curl up with an always-compelling Silhouette Romance novel and a refreshing glass of lemonade, and enjoy the summer!

Melissa Senate
Senior Editor
Silhouette Romance

Please address questions and book requests to:
Silhouette Reader Service
U.S.: 3010 Walden Ave., P.O. Box 1325, Buffalo, NY 14269
Canadian: P.O. Box 609, Fort Erie, Ont. L2A 5X3

HUSBAND IN RED

Cara Colter

Silhouette

R O M A N C E™

Published by Silhouette Books

America's Publisher of Contemporary Romance

For all the "angels" who helped

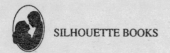 SILHOUETTE BOOKS

ISBN 0-373-19243-6

HUSBAND IN RED

This edition published by arrangement with Harlequin Books S.A.

® and TM are trademarks of Harlequin Books S.A., used under license. Trademarks indicated with ® are registered in the United States Patent and Trademark Office, the Canadian Trade Marks Office and in other countries.

Printed in U.S.A.

Books by Cara Colter

Silhouette Romance

Dare To Dream #491
Baby in Blue #1161
Husband in Red #1243

CARA COLTER

shares ten acres in the wild Kootenay region of British Columbia with the man of her dreams, three children, two horses, a cat with no tail and a golden retriever who answers best to "bad dog." She loves reading, writing and the woods in winter (no bears). She says life's delights include an automatic garage door opener and the skylight over the bed that allows her to see the stars at night.

She also says, "I have not lived a neat and tidy life, and used to envy those who did. Now I see my struggles as having given me a deep appreciation of life, and of love, that I hope I succeed in passing on through the stories that I tell."

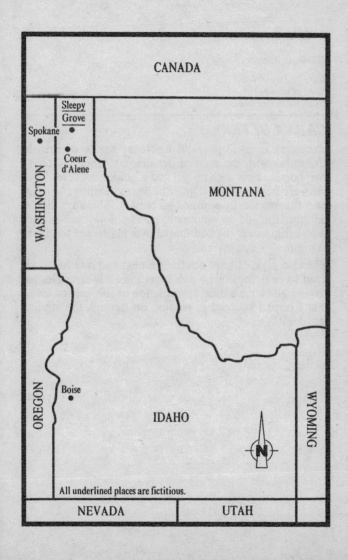

CANADA

Sleepy
Grove

Spokane

WASHINGTON

Coeur
d'Alene

MONTANA

OREGON

Boise

IDAHO

N

WYOMING

All underlined places are fictitious.

NEVADA   UTAH

Chapter One

"Auntie Angel, I have called 9-1-1."

Sadie McGee glanced up at her niece, and was struck again by the absolute beauty of the child with her tumbling black hair and somber gray eyes.

Too somber, Sadie thought distractedly. "You called what, Amber, honey?"

"9-1-1."

Her niece surely hadn't really called 9-1-1. Sadie wasn't even sure if the town of Sleepy Grove had 9-1-1. Years ago, when she'd lived here, the town had been small enough that if you just opened your front door and yelled "Help," half the populace came running.

"It's only a diaper," she told her niece. "I don't think I need 9-1-1." *Yet.* She realized the clothespin on her nose was not inspiring Amber's confidence, plus it was starting to pinch. She took it off and slid it into the pocket of the rumpled sweatpants she used for pajamas.

Her youngest nephew, Tyler, squirmed on the changing

table, gray eyes, identical to Amber's and every bit as somber, locked on Sadie.

Tucker, two and a half years old, with the same disconcerting gaze as his siblings, was also watching her. He, however, was underneath his bed. He had not moved from under that bed since his parents had left yesterday afternoon.

Sadie glanced at him. He disappeared deeper under the bed, but not before she saw the grimy tearstains on his cheeks and the peanut butter and jam smeared around his mouth.

At least he'd eaten the sandwich she'd put under the bed for him last night, she thought.

She sighed heavily. She was hopelessly unqualified for a two-week stint in child care. She'd tried to tell her brother, Mickey, and his wife, Samantha, that while she had nothing but love for her niece and nephews, she was not exactly a "kid" person. A university degree in commerce did not prepare one for the daily grind of—

"Auntie Angel!"

"I think I've got it!" Sadie said, pulling the plastic diaper tab into place and closing it. If she counted to ten and it didn't spring back open she was going to pronounce this a done deed.

Amber came and pulled urgently on her arm.

"Auntie Angel, I didn't call 9-1-1 about a diaper. I'm not a baby."

Sadie looked at her niece. She supposed five was not a baby anymore. In fact, there was a look so adult in her niece's eyes that it was troubling.

"I called 9-1-1 because the house is on fire."

Sadie froze, searching her niece's features for a glint of humor. Then she smelled the smoke.

She picked up the baby. The diaper fell off. Uncaring,

she thrust him into Amber's arms. She dove under the bed and grabbed wildly for Tucker. She got his ankle and hauled him out from under the bed. Heedless of his thrashing limbs, and his ear-piercing wail, she picked him up and pulled him in tight to her.

She put a hand over his mouth momentarily. "Follow me," she ordered Amber.

"We're supposed to crawl on the floor," Amber informed her. "Underneath the smoke."

Well, that made perfect sense if you weren't carrying babies and small children.

"Just follow me," she said with authoritative calm. Through the smoke she marched, down the hall and into the kitchen, past a flaming frying pan on the stove burner and out the back door.

Flaming frying pan? Sadie hardly considered herself awake yet, let alone ready to start breakfast.

She led the children to a spot near the big maple resplendent with fall colors. With one arm still firmly holding Tuck captive, she took the heavy baby from Amber's trembling, scrawny arms and set him firmly on the ground. She could hear sirens in the distance.

Amber sobbed, rubbing her eyes with tight fists.

"I didn't mean to. I was going to cook you bacon and eggs for breakfast," she wailed. "I didn't mean to!"

Sadie went down on her knees, and held out her free arm. Amber scrambled into her embrace.

"I didn't mean to!"

"Of course you didn't mean to, baby," Sadie soothed her. The sobs gave way to little choking sputters. Even Tuck settled down and patted his distraught sister on the head.

The sirens wailed closer.

Please, Sadie muttered heavenward, don't let *him* still be a firefighter on Sleepy Grove's volunteer brigade.

Which she realized was an awful waste of a prayer. She should probably be praying for her brother and sister-in-law's home.

She turned and looked back toward the house. It was a lovingly restored 1920s heritage building. Gray and white and single story, it had three covered verandas overlooking nearly an acre of yard. Inside were maple hardwood floors, replica period wallpapers, hand-stenciled borders, oak wainscotted walls. Her sister-in-law's warmth and charm were so evident in the decor and each piece of furniture.

"Are Daddy's paintings going to be hurt?" Amber asked, her sentence finishing with a sad hiccup.

Sadie felt her heart plunge to the ground. As if it wasn't bad enough that all Samantha's treasures were in danger of being destroyed. Mickey's paintings. How could she let anything happen to his paintings?

It was terrible enough that they were having to deal with the fact that kidney disease had struck Samantha.

Could Sadie really live with herself if the first time her brother and sister-in-law phoned home she told them their house—and the paintings—had burned to the ground while she stood outside and watched?

And what of the children? Would she move into a motel room with them? A nightmarish thought. What would it do to Amber to lose her home? Convince her irrevocably that the world was not a secure place? Make her feel like it wasn't safe to get too attached to anybody or anything?

No, she had to do something.

She set Tucker, calmer now, down on the ground and thrust his hand into Amber's. "Don't you let go of him, no matter what. And you, young man, stay here. Don't move an inch or I'll—'' What could she threaten him with? ''I'll leave Snappy in there.''

Tucker's eyes moved to the house. Thick smoke was billowing out the kitchen window. He stopped crying. ''Snappy.'' He whispered his discolored yellow bunny's name.

She didn't know he spoke, but now was not the time to contemplate it.

Baking soda, her mind was yelling at her as she headed back toward the house at a dead run.

The kitchen was very smoky, more oily flame roiling off that pan.

Who could have guessed one little pan of bacon and eggs could make so much smoke?

Coughing, her eyes watering, she opened cupboard doors, frantically searching. Finally, gagging, she found it. Triumphantly she turned the box over the flaming pan.

About a teaspoon of baking soda fell out and scattered ineffectually over the flames.

In a moment, she was sure the wall behind the stove, or the ceiling, was going to burst into flames.

She saw an oven mitt beside the stove. She could take the pan outside. Quickly she slid on the mitt. She reached for the pan.

And then she was shoved out of the way so brutally, she hit the floor.

Dazed she looked up to see a firefighter extinguishing the fire in the pan. The smoke thickened. Before she knew exactly what had happened, she had been picked up in a most undignified way and thrown over a strong, broad shoulder.

In a second she was outside, breathing in the beautiful crisp autumn air. She was tossed off that shoulder and laid, none too gently, on the ground.

She looked up at her rescuer, not with gratitude but with angry defiance. She wanted to tell him how utterly unnecessary his brutish show of strength had been. But when she opened her mouth, she realized she had swallowed more smoke than she had thought. Her throat felt raw, and her voice nonexistent.

He was resting on one knee of his bulky fire pants, and an oxygen mask hid his face.

If it was him, this would easily count as one of the world's most cruel coincidences. If it was him, this would easily count as the worst day of her entire life.

He pushed off the fire helmet. His hair was sweaty underneath it, but thick, dark and wavy as a fresh-turned row of loam.

Oh, no, she thought, catching her breath, as he pulled the oxygen mask away from his face.

It was him.

"Lady, what the hell were you thinking?"

He didn't recognize her. Well, of course he wouldn't recognize her. Seven years had gone by since he had seen her.

Seven years that had changed just about everything about her. The way she looked and the way she dressed and the way she talked.

And nothing had changed about him. Nothing. He still had the most gorgeous eyes she had ever seen—dark brown, glinting with sparks of gold, almond shaped and fringed with an impossible tangle of sooty lashes.

His face was lean and handsome, with dark slanting brows, a strong, straight nose, firm, sensuous lips, a hard chin.

When she'd seen him all those years ago, for the very first time, he'd taken her breath away. He had been—and still was—lethally attractive. If it wasn't enough that he possessed intriguing eyes and a perfectly sculpted face, he had the kind of body they put on posters these days.

He probably had posed for posters. Been Mr. July for a fireman's calendar that raised money for needy causes. He would have been standing there, all six feet plus of him, stripped to the waist, to better show off his lean, hard body, the promise of easy and unforced strength in the soot-smudged bulges at his biceps, the rock-hard contours of his chest.

She was just guessing, of course, what his naked chest would look like, because he'd been fully clothed, and stayed that way for the duration of their relationship, if what had passed between them could even qualify for that term.

Now he seemed to have matured to have even greater breadth across his shoulders and depth across his chest.

She could tell even though he wore the cumbersome fire jacket. He still took her breath away. It was coming in heated, ragged gasps right now, though hopefully it was only because he had so ungraciously slammed her into the ground.

He looked faintly angry now, just as he had when they had said goodbye for the final time.

Those All-American-boy good looks disappeared into something very dangerous looking when his brow and the corners of his mouth turned down.

"You were going to try and take the pan out of the house, weren't you?"

His voice sent a tingle down her spine. Was it deeper than it had been? Was there an edge of steel in his voice that had not been there before?

If she had any sense of self-preservation, she would deny she had planned to pick up that pan. He looked as if he planned to shake her.

But there wasn't much that Sadie McGee had backed down from in her life, and now was no time to start, even if her voice had conveniently fled her. She nodded vehemently.

"Do you have any idea what you would have looked like if some of that grease splashed on to you?"

She shook her head. She forced her voice to work, though it was a humiliating croak. "My sister-in-law's treasures—"

He grunted impatiently. "I know what you would have looked like, and let me tell you—"

"Is Auntie Angel all right?"

He stopped, and looked at Amber who had materialized at his right elbow, with Tucker's hand still in hers and the baby awkwardly balanced on one small hip. She was panting with exertion, her face salt-streaked with tear stains.

In a gesture completely natural, he took the baby from Amber, set it on his thigh and rested back on his heels. "Sure, sweetheart, your aunt is fine." It did not even seem possible that the gaze that returned with such piercing intensity to Sadie's face belonged to the same man as did that gentle voice.

"These," he said sternly and quietly, "are your sister-in-law's treasures."

Looking at him now brought the sting of tears to Sadie's eyes.

She wasn't upset by the fact that there had not even been a glimmer of recognition in his eyes.

Or the fact that he looked so wonderful with that baby, all his masculine strength tempered by the gentleness with which he held Tyler.

Or the fact that the man she'd dreamed about for untold hours of her young adulthood was now reprimanding her as if she were a wayward child.

How long after that ill-fated relationship had she tormented herself by imagining him dangling babies—their babies—in his arms?

How long had she sat by a phone that never rang? Even though she had told him not to call, a part of her had wanted him not to believe her, not to listen.

How long had she imagined if she just had another chance she could make herself over to fit into his world?

Of course, she'd been young, so young and childish back then. She looked deliberately away from the cool intensity of his eyes, and stared up at the sky.

She had just known she should never come back to Sleepy Grove.

She had told him that at their last meeting. That Sleepy Grove was not in her plans. That she would *never* come back here.

Older now, she knew all about the word *never*. Using it was like challenging the gods.

"If Auntie Angel's okay," Amber asked him evenly, "why is she crying?"

Sadie snuck a peek at him.

He did not look in the least sympathetic. "Hopefully," he muttered, "she's just beginning to realize how serious a mistake she made back there."

Still, he was watching her closely, faint puzzlement beginning to edge out professional scrutiny.

"Do I know you?" he finally asked.

"No," she said tersely, her voice still a croak. Well, good, that wouldn't give her away, either. She forced herself to sit up, then swiped impatiently at the tear that cascaded down her nose. "You don't."

And it was true. He didn't.

Seven years ago, Sadie's wonderful friend, Kate Shea, had purchased a date with him, by accident, at the town's

first annual bachelor auction. Kate had been madly in love
with Hawk Adams, and Sadie had gone on the date instead.

It had been an astonishing experience. She had been prepared to have great fun on her gift date with Michael
O'Bryan, picturing herself as a good sport going along with
a great gag. But nobody had warned her what he looked
like.

And then she had wanted so badly to be liked by him
that, in her mind, everything went wrong. She was tongue-
tied when he asked her a question, and sharp-tongued when
she tried to be funny.

And he had been Mr. Charm. Acting as if he really liked
her. Laughing in all the right places. Taking her hand and
staring at her with a sizzling intensity that threatened to
catch her nether regions on fire.

And, of course, she had fallen for him hopelessly.

Because he was so good-looking, and so effortlessly
charming, and so out of her reach and her league.

He'd been living in Sleepy Grove at the time, and she'd
been in Spokane, working at a seedy bar until college
started in the fall.

He'd actually phoned her. Long-distance. Three times in
one week. And then come to see her again the following
weekend. He'd actually taken her, Sadie McGee, on a date
because he wanted to. He'd shown up early Sunday afternoon and taken her to fly a kite in the park. She'd never
flown a kite before. And after, he'd taken her to the best
restaurant in all of Spokane.

There had been more long distance calls and then she
had made her fatal mistake. She had gone to see him in
Sleepy Grove.

Sleepy Grove. Small Town, America, with its shady
boulevards, old brick buildings downtown and its town
square with wrought-iron benches and old men playing

chess. Sleepy Grove, with storefronts under bright awnings, and people calling greetings to each other across uncrowded streets, and swings creaking on porches at night.

That was his Sleepy Grove.

Hers was a house on the wrong side of the tracks—a weedy lawn, with a dismantled car in front of a house the porch was falling off of. Oh yes, she was one of *those* McGees, the wrong-side-of-the-track McGees.

And she had never felt the mantle of it more strongly than when Michael O'Bryan, clean-cut and fresh-faced, son of one of the town's more prominent families had come to call.

He'd taken her to a movie and out for a soda after, and people had stared.

He didn't seem to notice, but the more they stared the harder she had become.

When he'd dropped her off, her dad, drunk as usual, had had lots to say about giving herself airs and who did she think she was.

Michael had called her the next day, and asked her if she wanted to come over to his place for a swim.

The O'Bryan place. A great big perfectly maintained and manicured mansion and estate in the most exclusive part of town. For a swim.

Not even the lure of seeing him in swim trunks could have got her there. She'd told him then she was going back to Spokane and that she was never coming back here.

To this place where her past was in her face all the time. Where people judged her by where she came from instead of who she was. Where she judged herself without mercy and found herself not worthy of someone like him.

Naturally, she resented the hell out of *him* for that, as insensible as that was. Love was not sensible.

After two weeks, she knew that.

She knew he would never leave here, and she could never stay here.

Even after she was dreadful to him, she somehow hoped he wouldn't believe her. That he'd call. That he'd still come see her in Spokane, but never ask her to come back here.

It all seemed rather foolish now that the wrong-side-of-the-track McGees were making something of themselves. Mickey owned, outright, one of the nicest houses in Sleepy Grove. He had paintings in corporate collections. The president of the United States of America had just commissioned a work from him. He was married—happily—to Dr. Height's daughter.

And yet with all his success, Mickey was still just Mickey. He still wore his hair too long, and an earring in one ear; he slopped around town driving his same old green truck, and wearing jeans with the knees out, and plaid logger's shirts.

Anybody who knew him seven years ago would still know him today.

But the person she had been seven years ago was gone, and she thought that was something to be thankful for.

She'd been a gum-popping girl, who wore her skirts too short, her hair bleached blond and her makeup too thick.

She didn't bleach her hair anymore. Or wear miniskirts. She hardly ever chewed gum. Her makeup was applied with a light and expert hand.

Plus, Sadie McGee, the girl who'd struggled through high school with a straight C average, had an honors degree in commerce and was one of the fastest rising stars in the biggest public-relations firm in Seattle. Kevin Wyn-Wilde, a handsome, young and ambitious lawyer she had met through her firm, had just asked her to marry him.

"This is my Auntie Angel," Amber introduced Sadie gravely to Michael.

Michael nodded to her. "Angel."

She could have corrected him. She could have told him "Angel" had been Amber's baby way of saying Sadie, and somehow it had stuck.

But she didn't want him to know that she'd been that vulnerable girl he'd taken on a paid date once a long time ago. She didn't want to resurrect their short and painful past. She wanted to do her duty to her brother, take care of a little business her firm had here and then leave, unscathed.

"Auntie Angel's baby-sitting, 'cause my mommy's real sick. I'm Amber McGee."

She held out her small hand to him, and Sadie saw the tiny smile tug at his lips before being carefully repressed.

He changed the baby to the other thigh, and shook Amber's hand just as gravely as she had offered it.

"How do you do?" he said to her. "I'm Michael O'Bryan."

"You live across the street, don't you?"

"Yes, in the yellow house."

He lived on the same street, Sadie thought, groaning inwardly. She should have known better than to come back here.

"Do you live all by yourself?" Amber asked.

I don't care, I don't care, I don't care, Sadie chanted to herself, but it seemed like her whole body was absolutely rigid waiting for his answer.

"Yeah, I do."

Did he slide just the tiniest little look her way?

She remembered with mortification she was wearing her oldest sweatpants, and the oversize flannel shirt she preferred for pajamas. She knew for a fact she hadn't combed her hair yet today, and she probably had baby gunk on her sleeve.

"My dad's name is Michael, too," Amber said, "but everybody calls him Mickey. This is my brother Tucker. He's very shy, but he wants to be a volunteer firefighter someday, too, don't you, Tuck?"

Tuck peeked out from behind Amber, pulled his thumb out of his mouth and nodded vigorously.

"Tell you what, Amber, if you get your baby-sitter to bring you down to the station, I'll show you and Tucker around."

I am not a baby-sitter, Sadie cried inwardly. *I'm a powerful woman executive.*

Still, she saw the enthusiastic light that lit Amber's eyes. For a moment she looked like a happy little girl, not a worried miniature grown-up.

"Could we, Auntie Angel?"

She could not put out that light in her niece's face. "Of course," she said, but she was already plotting diversionary tactics. She could probably talk Amber into a trade. A trip to Silverwood, the amusement park, instead of a tour of the fire hall.

"If you have a kitchen fire again," Michael told Sadie, "put it out with baking soda, or cover the pan with a lid. Even if you just leave it, it will usually burn itself out. But never, ever try to move the pan. Okay?"

He stood up then, shifting the baby easily. He handled the baby with a degree of comfort that was unnerving. He was at an age now where some of his girlfriends would have children. Women had always adored him, thrown themselves at him. Of course she knew, from the occasional very casual inquiry, that he had never married.

He looked very tall and intimidating, and Sadie scrambled to her feet.

He still looked tall and intimidating. He must be six feet

tall, or maybe a little more. She, sadly, was only an inch over five. She drew herself to her full height, anyway.

"It's not likely to happen again," she said with regal annoyance.

"That's right," Amber said, her hand creeping into Sadie's. "Never again."

"How did it happen?"

Just a question, but there was something in the way that little hand tightened around hers that practically begged Sadie not to tell the fireman who had started the fire.

And, really, he didn't even know who she was. She didn't have to impress him with how capable she was, especially not at Amber's expense.

"A moment's inattention" was all she said.

She felt the full force of his gaze then, warm brown eyes flecked with gold, and she actually saw understanding dawn in them.

And she remembered how she had come to care about him so much in so short a time when, instead of looking at Amber, instead of lecturing her on the danger of fire and little hands, he turned away from them both and studied the house.

"It's a beautiful house, but in these situations the house is the last thing I worry about."

Those eyes on her face again, warm laughter lurking somewhere in them.

Oh, how she remembered his laughter. How she'd loved making him laugh!

But it would be a mistake to think he'd been worried about her. A compassionate kind of guy. Well, tell it to somebody who hadn't sat by the phone for two years waiting for him to call.

It was irrelevant, in her mind, that she was the one who'd told him not to call.

She let go of Amber's hand and held out her arms for the baby, a gesture that clearly said goodbye.

Michael handed him over, but not before lifting Tyler high above his head and making him squeal with delight.

As soon as Tyler was in her arms, she felt a warm wet circle widen on her shirt. She stared down at Tyler in dismay.

Michael threw back his head and laughed.

For a moment, Sadie stared at him, completely mesmerized by the sound of his laughter, completely unprepared for how his teeth flashed, brilliant and white, making him look even more handsome than he had looked before.

She thought she'd remembered.

Memories, even ones that haunted for far longer than the actual experience warranted, did not hold a candle to the real thing.

His laughter stopped, but the warmth lingered. She had to close her eyes against the yearning that reared up within her, an angry dragon that had not been tamed after all. A wanting so fierce, it could have scorched her.

When she opened her eyes, he was scooping his helmet and oxygen mask off the ground. He gave her a small salute, accompanied by a half smile that also stabbed deep into her memory, and then he turned away from them and strode across the yard.

The fire trucks pulled out of the yard a few minutes later, and the curious neighbors began to disperse.

Sadie had been given instructions to phone the insurance company about minor smoke damage.

She led her little flock back into the house and poured cereal into bowls. The house smelled terrible but the damage seemed minimal—a few sooty smoke smudges on the ceiling above the stove and on some of the cupboards and walls.

When they were all settled—Tyler, strapped into his high chair gleefully throwing Cheerios on the floor, Tucker re-united with Snappy under the bed, and Amber studying the pictures on the back of the cereal box—Sadie slipped into the bathroom and shut the door.

She closed her eyes, took a deep breath and then opened them to look appraisingly at herself in the full-length mirror mounted on the back of the door.

"Good grief," she said with a sigh.

It was worse than she thought. A dark smudge of soot, the width of a paintbrush, ran under her left eye, over the bridge of her nose and finished with a dark charcoal splotch by her jawline.

Michael O'Bryan hadn't recognized her? Her own brother probably would have walked by her on the street!

The sweatpants hung baggily, the crotch in the unfortu-nate vicinity of her knees. The flannel shirt swam around her, the big wet blotch dead center. Not a curve showing there.

She looked absolutely shapeless, and if that wasn't bad enough, her hair, recently cut shorter, was standing straight up on end, looking exactly like porcupine quills. Not even the expensive highlights she'd had added to her natural sandy brown color showed to any advantage. Savagely, she yanked an invading twig and a bright red maple leaf from her hair.

Okay, hair, clothes, smudge aside, what had Michael O'Bryan seen?

She studied herself critically, and sighed again. She had lovely eyes, undoubtedly her best feature, but without even a touch of makeup, even they didn't look that great at half past eight in the morning.

Her nose was turned up, and her mouth was too small.

"Rosebud lips" Mickey had said once when he was sketching her.

She had that sketch somewhere. She was sitting on a log, and she looked like a little woodland leprechaun.

She was willing to bet Michael O'Bryan didn't date little woodland leprechauns.

She was willing to bet he dated tall, slender girls with curves that showed even if they were wearing flannel shirts, which they wouldn't be. No, Michael O'Bryan would date girls who slept in little lace teddies.

Those kind of women who had looked down their long straight noses at her when she had sat sipping a Coke with him in the Sleepy Grove Emporium of Fine Eats after the movie he'd taken her to. One, a girl who had been two years ahead of her in high school, and had been voted most likely to become a flight attendant in the high school annual, had even waited until he'd gone to the men's room and then sidled over with a mean glint in her eye.

"How'd *you* manage this?" Lizette Mallory had asked incredulously.

"Wouldn't you like to know?" Sadie had snapped back, the roughness of her tone hiding the slice to her heart.

Not good enough. From the wrong side of town. Every one of her insecurities—and there were many of them—surfaced, but she pushed them down deep where this witch was never going to see them.

"Well," Lizette had said, her eyes sliding toward Michael as he walked over to rejoin them, "no use breaking your heart over what you can't have."

And then she'd proceeded to stand there and talk to him, as if Sadie wasn't there!

She wondered why she was wasting her time caring what kind of girl Michael O'Bryan dated *now*.

She scrunched her nose at herself in the mirror. "The

big oaf had his chance at you," she told her reflection. "He missed it. His loss."

Or maybe she had that wrong. She'd had her chance at him. And been afraid of all that meant. Staying forever in a small town where she didn't feel she could ever hold her head up high.

She snorted at herself. "Girl, you were a temporary diversion to him. The word *forever* never came up."

Because she hadn't allowed it to?

"Idiot. You weren't the kind of girl he was going to settle down with. You knew it and cut your losses early."

"Auntie Angel, are you talking to somebody?"

"No," she called. He hadn't settled down with anybody. A case in point. Still, seeing him again had stirred something in her. Something that had not been stirred for a long time.

Somewhere, she had a diary of those days of that painful schoolgirl crush she'd had for him.

It was probably in the same box of memories as that leprechaun sketch.

But she didn't need the diary to remind her of the pain of leaving that weekend, knowing she was never coming back.

Knowing he certainly wasn't coming after her.

And knowing it was for the best. They were from two different worlds. A unicorn didn't spend his life with a burro, and there was no doubting who was who in that equation.

She'd thrown herself into her studies that fall, and discovered a whole new side to Sadie McGee.

Whether it was a lack of distractions, or being away from her crazy family, or just Kate Shea's simple faith in her, she'd excelled at college. She'd begun to feel the power in education and knowledge, and she drank it greedily as though she'd grown up in the desert.

Oh, there were men. Boys, really. Classmates who she joined for pizza and movies and study sessions. But none who distracted her from the delicious discoveries about herself and what she was capable of.

And the guys she had dated were all the most ordinary of men. As soon as she saw a man who made her heart do funny things, she deliberately avoided him.

And then Kevin Wyn-Wilde had come along. He was a lawyer doing some legal work for her firm. They'd started dating about a year ago. He was handsome and ambitious. He came from one of Seattle's oldest families. Last week he had taken her completely by surprise by asking her to marry him.

Take that Lizette Mallory.

She couldn't answer him. She wasn't even sure why. So, he'd given her some big rock that was a family heirloom, and that was too big for her, and told her to think about it while she was away.

Sadie knew she didn't love him, but she was no great believer in love, anyway. To her, love equalled pain, and there was no room in this new life of hers for pain.

But there were different kinds of pain in the world, and for the last three years her sister-in-law had been ill.

Her sister-in-law, the beautiful girl who had always had everything. Exactly the kind of girl Michael O'Bryan should have ended up with. The cheerleader, the doctor's daughter.

The girl Sadie had come to love like her own sister.

Sadie had sworn never to go back to Sleepy Grove. Never. There were too many people here who knew who and what she once had been.

Even when Mickey and Sam started having the kids, she

didn't come back, satisfying herself with the photographs they sent, then joining them in Coeur d'Alene for holidays every year.

But those family ties were so strong. And right now her family needed her. By an odd twist in fate, the PR firm she worked for was representing a company interested in building a strip mall here on a piece of land being made available by the town. Her job would be to do the proposal to get the site—where a turn-of-the-century fire hall now sat—signed, sealed and delivered.

"Auntie Angel, Tucker spilled chocolate milk underneath the bed," Amber said from outside the door.

She took one last look at herself.

She didn't look much like Ms. McGee, marketing executive for Herbert, Lamb and Butterfield right now.

For now, she was just Auntie Angel, baby-sitter.

And if her first morning on the job was any indication, she was in big trouble.

Chapter Two

"Can we go on a tour of the fire hall tomorrow?" Amber asked.

Sadie was discovering her niece had the face of an angel and the tenacity of a bulldog.

Three days had passed since the "fire." Amber had mentioned the fire hall twenty-three times before Sadie gave up and stopped counting.

Tonight, Amber was in candy-floss pink pajamas, her thick dark hair tied back with a ribbon. She smelled of soap and sleepiness, and Sadie felt an almost physical stab of yearning.

"I'm too young for my biological clock to be ticking," she thought out loud.

"Twenty-four isn't young." Amber cocked her head and regarded her aunt thoughtfully. "It's quite old actually. What's a logical clock?"

Sadie resisted, barely, the urge to run to the nearest mirror and see what new telltale wrinkle or sag had led her niece to pronounce her "quite old."

"I was just thinking out loud. It was nothing really. Grown-up stuff."

"Can we go to the fire hall tomorrow. Please?"

Unless she was mistaken, unshed tears lit the back of Amber's eyes. There was a degree of desperation in her voice that hadn't been there before, and Sadie realized she hadn't been the only one counting the number of requests.

"I was thinking we might take a drive down to Silverwood." Her diversionary tactics were not working. Time for the big guns. The offer to go to the theme park was a measure of her own desperation. An amusement park with one adult and three children under six would probably be an exhausting and exasperating undertaking.

"We could ask Kate if she wants to bring Ethan and Becky," she suggested to Amber in a flash of inspiration.

"Ethan Adams is very much a pain," Amber announced formally. "Just because he's three months older than me, he tries to boss me around. Besides, I think Silverwood is closed for the year. I don't want to go there without my mom, anyway. She said she'd take me next year when she's feeling better."

Sadie studied her niece suspecting, suddenly, Amber had decided not to do anything fun until her mom came back to do it with her.

"Your mom would want you to have fun, Amber."

Amber shook her head stubbornly. "How can I have fun when my mom's sick? My heart is sick with her."

Sadie felt a quick prick of tears behind her own eyes.

"The fire hall isn't fun," Amber said. "It's education. I don't understand why *you* don't want to go."

Sadie could hardly explain to Amber she didn't want to see Michael O'Bryan again. He awakened some strangely savage emotion in her, better left sleeping. The very sight of him made Kevin Wyn-Wilde seem like an old sepia photograph fading away to nothing.

"Did you like him?" Amber asked shrewdly.

"Who?" Sadie yelped.

"Michael O'Bryan."

"Really, Amber, there was nothing to like or dislike about him—"

"I thought he was ever so handsome. Not quite as good-looking as my dad, but next best."

"Well, I'm sure he'd be the first to agree with you," Sadie said hastily, wondering how to turn this wayward conversation around. "You know, going to see the fire station *is* educational. In fact, you'll probably be going to visit with your kindergarten class. You don't want to spoil the surprise, do you?"

"Tucker won't get to go with my class. Tucker really wants to go. He'll even come out from underneath the bed. I'd like to go twice."

Sadie wanted to ask her how she knew she'd like to go twice when she hadn't even been there once yet, but she could see that for some reason this meant a lot to Amber.

If it brought a sparkle into those serious eyes, shouldn't Sadie be willing to make the sacrifice? If, for a while, it made that little heart forget to be sick, wouldn't it be worth any price she had to pay?

If just the sight of Michael O'Bryan made her think Kevin seemed like a worn-out old photo, fading fast from memory, wasn't that something she needed to know?

If it got Tucker out from underneath the bed, that would a slight payoff, wouldn't it?

Michael O'Bryan would think she'd fallen for him if she showed up at his place of work so soon.

"So can we?"

"How about if I phone and see when it would be convenient for us to go?'' Perhaps, with a little scheming, a time that would be convenient for them would be coincidentally inconvenient for him.

Amber smiled. ''Thanks, Auntie Angel. You're an angel.'' And then she giggled, and that sound almost made it worth it for Sadie to swallow her pride.

''Hey, O'Bryan.''

Twenty-five. With a grunt of exertion Michael lifted the weight back onto its rest. His arms ached. He could feel the blood pumping through his muscles, and the sweat trickling down his bare chest.

''Yeah?''

''Remember that grease fire we were on a couple of days ago?''

Since that had been the only fire the volunteer department had been called out on in the past week, Michael remembered it quite well. ''Sure, I remember,'' he said, watching his friend and fellow volunteer Murphy come into the fire hall's weight room.

''*She* just called.''

He sat up and looked at the other fireman with interest. Angel. Last night after work, when he'd driven by her house on his way home, they'd been outside, Angel and the children, playing in the leaves in the front yard. Well, Angel had been playing in the leaves, the little girl watching solemnly as her aunt tried to convince her to jump.

He'd slowed his vehicle to a crawl, and watched Angel cavorting in those leaves, leaping and tumbling and burying herself in them, and throwing them over her head.

He couldn't quite make out her facial features, but he'd suspected there was a figure under that scarecrow outfit she'd been wearing the day of the fire, and he'd been right.

Last night she'd been dressed in blue jeans that showed

off the slenderness of her legs and the delicious roundness of her bottom.

She'd had on a flannel jacket, but it was open over a form-fitting T-shirt, and surprise, surprise, Angel had form.

Her hair had looked about the same, sticking up every which way, but he liked it. She looked wholesome and natural with her cheeks flushed and leaves sticking out of her hair. A part of him sure would have liked to go play in the leaves with her. In fact, a part of him had felt, *again,* some strange flicker of recognition.

He'd looked at Amber again. Even from a distance, she looked forlorn standing on the edge of those inviting heaps of fall colors. He could tell she wanted to play, but wouldn't let herself. Poor little thing. The whole town knew her mom had been sick for a long time. That really did a number on kids.

He noticed the baby sitting to one side, happily cramming leaves in his mouth. He didn't see the other little boy right away, and then spotted him, still in the house, his solemn round face pressed to the window.

"You know, the cute one," Murphy said, when Michael didn't answer him right away.

"And?" He kept his voice carefully neutral. He was beginning to feel a bit suspicious. Murphy seemed almost…gleeful.

"She wants to bring the kids for a tour."

"That's great," Michael said. "It's always good PR to show kids through. That's why I invited her to bring them by someday."

Inside, he was wondering if it meant something that that day was so soon. Had she felt that same little tug of interest in him that he had felt in her?

"I know you invited her," Murphy crowed. "That's why it's so funny that she asked when you *wouldn't* be here."

And then Murphy cracked up laughing as though it was the greatest joke in the world.

"She asked when I wouldn't be here?" Michael felt a little tingle of surprise...and intrigue. He reached for his navy blue T-shirt with the firefighter emblem on the breast. "Maybe—" he passed his hand lightly over a network of fine scars on his chest and neck "—she caught a little glimpse of these."

"Look, Michael, take it from a guy with red hair and freckles and arms the size of toothpicks, women *never* ask when you won't be around. And those—" he gestured at the scars "—just seem to add to the appeal. *Cop hurt in wild car chase.* Just gets them. My wife slobbers over you, for heaven's sake. That's why I thought it was so great that there's one out there who isn't interested. Not even a little bit. Now you know how the rest of us feel."

He hadn't just been hurt in that car chase, Michael corrected his friend mentally. His career had ended. The scars had healed, but his back never would. It wasn't that he couldn't be active—the very opposite. He couldn't be *inactive.* Long periods of sitting in a car or behind a desk nearly killed him. He was thirty years old and had been offered a pension. It was disgusting.

"How did you manage to catch Karen when you're so positively repulsive?" Michael asked Murphy dryly.

"Personality," Murphy told him happily. "Brains. Charm. Wit—"

"Okay, sorry I asked already."

"When is the last time you went out with somebody?" Murphy asked.

"Last Saturday," Michael said.

Murphy snorted. "See, you still have it. Different girl every night, I suppose."

"Something like that."

Michael O'Bryan didn't tell lies. He had gone out with somebody last Saturday. He'd picked his mother up and taken her for groceries.

And there wasn't a different girl every night. There hadn't been for a long, long time. But he'd discovered how easy it was to ward off the well-meaning matchmakers in this too-small-town by saying the right word at the right time.

In truth, Michael hadn't been on a date in longer than he could remember. But he'd done enough of that in his younger days to last him a lifetime. And to give him a reputation that apparently was going to last him a lifetime, too.

He was pretty sure that in his late teens and early twenties he'd wined and dined and danced with every available woman in northern Idaho.

And then he'd been burned in the accident, and his back injured beyond repair, and something had changed in him. The injury had forced him to look at life in a different way, and to see himself in a different light.

He'd bought a little house that was nearly falling down and nursed it back to life. He had a knack for renovations, and he'd made good money when he sold the house. The one he was in now was the third one he'd revitalized. His firefighter friends would probably be astounded to know he had never entertained an overnight visitor there.

Now he was ready for a bigger project, and he'd been eyeing the old town fire hall for some time. He'd already talked to an old friend about leasing part of it for a restaurant, after he'd completed the renovations, a project he thought would probably take him at least a year, given the disreputable state the lovely old building had been allowed to fall into.

The other part he was going to use to sell handmade

wooden fire trucks. While he'd been recuperating from the accident—a long and frustrating period—he'd saved his sanity by reviving the Volunteer Fireman's Christmas Toy Campaign. Most toys these days couldn't be fixed up, but some of them could. He fixed the ones that could be fixed to look brand-new. And he began to make wooden fire engines, each year the design becoming a little more intricate, a little more sophisticated.

Nobody was more surprised than he was when collectors began to approach him about his creations, and offered him astronomical amounts for them. It soon became apparent to him he'd be further ahead selling the trucks and buying the kids bicycles.

So, he hadn't had a date in two years. He hadn't really missed it, either.

But it was something of a slap in the face that the first woman he'd even been remotely interested in for a long time had turned him down flat—before he even had a chance to ask.

It reminded him of a girl a long time ago....

"What's that frown about?" Murphy asked with a hoot. "Is someone about to die?"

Michael shook his head to clear the image, and stood up abruptly.

"Where you going?" Murphy asked him.

"To change my shift," he said with an evil grin.

It wasn't because he liked her, he told himself. How did he know if he liked her or not? It would take a long time to know something like that. He was no longer the young man who had decided whether or not he liked someone on the basis of how they looked and how they dressed and what they drove.

She'd changed all that. Years ago. A girl who had looked all wrong, but been so right. Funny, outrageous, original.

She'd dumped him cold.

He felt a funny shiver go up and down his spine. The grease fire had been at Mickey McGee's. The girl, so familiar, and yet not. It might be a sister, he realized, and suddenly, against his will, he longed for news of Sadie.

She could be anywhere by now, doing anything. He never had asked Mickey, or their other mutual friends Hawk and Kate Adams, either, because word might have gotten back to her that he had. But he'd wondered. She was a girl who was going to set the world on fire, and he was the guy who would have given anything to stop her. To hoard her fire all to himself.

She'd wrecked him nearly as badly as the accident had, truth be known.

Because she had shone, and everything else had seemed dull and tarnished in comparison to her.

He wanted to know *why* this other girl, who bore some troubling resemblance to Sadie, didn't want to see him. Was it because he'd lectured her about burning frying pans? Had the scars on his neck revolted her? Maybe there was even the possibility she was attracted to him and attached to someone else.

But the bottom line was this—if it was going to make her damned uncomfortable that he was going to be here, then he was going to be here.

The second she stepped into the fire hall, he knew.

She didn't look like Sadie, but she was Sadie.

Everything about her was different—her hair and her makeup and the way she dressed. She actually looked even less like the Sadie of his memory than she had the morning of the fire.

But there was something about the way she was standing there in the fire hall's tiny administration office, the children at her side and the baby snoozing in a colorful stroller beside them, that called to his heart.

Hello. It's me again.

There was the faintest touch of insecurity around her, as if at any moment, she expected someone to come and ask her to leave.

Her hair fell in soft, feathery wisps around her face, light brown, gold where the overhead light touched it. She had used a dusting of makeup today, and her eyes looked huge, forget-me-not blue. Her mouth, pink and faintly parted in surprise, looked like a kissable little bow.

But most surprising of all was how sophisticated she looked dressed as she was in a straight-line navy skirt and jacket, and a soft ivory long-sleeved blouse that he was positive was silk. High heels had added at least an inch to her height. She now almost reached the bottom of his chin.

She looked lovely, slender and willowy. He wasn't quite sure how someone so short had managed to make her legs look long, but she had.

It occurred to him he wasn't supposed to be here, so who had she dressed so pleasingly for?

With just a touch of hesitation she accepted his out-stretched hand.

Her hand was tiny inside his, delicately soft and lusciously warm, something he remembered. But her handshake was surprisingly strong and businesslike.

For a moment he didn't know what to do. Play along with her? Pretend he didn't remember? Call her Angel as if she was brand new to him? As if they had never chased each other over the green hills of a park, a kite dancing on the wind behind them?

But he found he couldn't do that.

"Sadie," he said, and the single word came off his lips loaded with memories he had not intended for it to hold.

Her chin shot up, and pride flashed in her eyes. "Michael."

"I can't believe I didn't recognize you the other morning."

She laughed, even though he could tell she didn't want to. Her laugh had been tamed somewhat, not robust and wild around the edges the way it used to be.

"I might have been offended if you did recognize me that day!"

"Why didn't you tell me?"

Silence. She studied the sleeping baby for a moment, then looked back at him. "I guess I was rattled...from the fire."

"Look at you now," he said, but he felt a little sad when he looked at her. She used to wear a little too much makeup, and her hair had been a little on the brassy side. The first time he'd met her, she'd had on a black leather skirt so short, it had taken his breath away. Not his kind of girl at all, and yet after a few minutes, he hadn't remembered the makeup or the hair—the skirt was not so easily dismissed. The girl had a spark so strong, dry tinder would have ignited around her.

Now she was sophisticated, the brassiness gone, her hair perfect, her makeup perfect, her skirt schoolmarm proper. But where was the spark? She looked cool, polished, sophisticated.

She had been the kind of girl, he had thought, way back when, who would ride camels across searing deserts, wrestle alligators, lead safaris.

He'd let her go to become this? Little Miss Boardroom U.S.A.?

Still, it was an act of discipline to release her hand. When he did he noticed the flash of light on her left hand.

Unable to stop himself he picked her hand up, and examined the huge ring that glittered there.

"You're engaged?" With a lot of effort he made his voice sound as if he didn't care, as if he were just an old acquaintance mildly interested. Of course, he should have dropped her hand right away if that was the impression he meant to give.

She grabbed her hand from his and stuffed it behind her back, like a little kid caught wearing her mother's ring.

"It's—it's not official yet," she stammered, a bit of her polish scraped.

He was mean enough to be glad. He thought the ring was very ugly and ostentatious. It hadn't been sized for her, and looked too large.

"What exactly does that mean, *not official yet?*" he pressed.

She glared at him. He was making her mad, and he liked that, too. A little hissing kitten behind that polished mask would please him to no end.

"I mean," he persisted silkily, "are you waiting to fall for him *officially* at some later date?"

Her hand curled up into a small fist at her side.

She's going to smack me, he thought with glee. That would be more like the Sadie he'd known. Wind up and smack some guy up the side of his head for putting her on the spot.

But to his disappointment her hand uncurled. In a very modulated voice she said, "We're both juggling busy careers right now."

He considered saying something about real passion not taking the back seat to a career, but decided to back off. There was no sense making her really mad at him—especially since things weren't official yet.

"I hope he's a nice guy," he said with utter insincerity.

Actually, he didn't hope that at all. He hoped he was a
complete ass, and if things did become *official* that her
marriage lasted three weeks, and that she came home to
Sleepy Grove and handed her broken heart to him for repair
when it was all over.

Which was ridiculous. He hadn't seen her in seven years.
They'd had a two-week relationship. If it could even be
called that.

He saw her eyes find the scars on his neck. She hadn't
even come when he'd been clinging to life by a thread.

The girl hadn't cared about him. The girl had had plans.
And now she stood here before him, the woman she had
planned to be.

"He is," she said. "A nice guy, a lawyer."

He wasn't exactly sure that those two terms could be
used together in the same sentence, but he bit his tongue
and turned to Amber and Tucker.

"Thank you for coming. I've been looking forward to
your visit."

"You know my aunt!" Amber said.

"We were friends a long time ago."

"Aren't you still friends?" Amber demanded.

He looked at Sadie, this different Sadie, who wore silk
and was going to marry a lawyer, and didn't look much
like she'd ever chased through a park flying a kite, laughing
until tears left funny little black streaks all over her cheeks.

"I don't know," he said honestly, and was surprised and
just a touch satisfied to see Sadie flinch.

Amber had obviously dressed as carefully as her aunt,
and he focussed on her deliberately. "I like polka dots,"
he confided in her.

She beamed with pleasure.

"Tucker," he said, extending his hand, "good to see
you."

Tucker darted out from behind Amber, gave Michael's hand one vigorous and slightly sticky shake and went back into hiding.

"We even got him out from under the bed to have a bath," Amber informed him confidentially.

"Out from under the bed?"

She nodded. "He's been living under his bed since Mommy and Daddy left."

"Isn't that quite some time ago?"

"Nearly a week."

Out of the corner of his eye, he could see Sadie studying a CPR poster on the wall as if it had been executed by Michelangelo.

Her chin was tilted upward at a proud angle, and he knew it would probably be best to let this topic drop, but curiosity got the best of him.

"Doesn't he come out to eat?"

"We thought he would," Amber said, "but after a while when he didn't, Auntie Angel started putting his plate under there for him."

Auntie Angel, he saw, had leaned closer to that poster. Tucker staying under the bed was a sore point with Ms. Chairman of the Board.

"Kids do odd things, don't they?" he asked. He wanted to tell her it wasn't her fault the kid was under the bed, but her face wasn't exactly inviting sympathy or camaraderie, either.

He gave them the royal deluxe tour of the small fire hall. That included letting Amber and Tucker turn on the lights on the truck, and the siren, very briefly. He helped the kids into the heavy fireman's jackets, and boots, and helmets. They giggled under the enormous weight. He slid down the pole from the dormitory to the truck six times before they were satisfied.

He kept sliding Sadie glances. She looked icily remote, and he thought he must have imagined that faint aura of insecurity when he'd first seen her.

"Do you want to stay for lunch?" he said on an impulse when it became apparent to him that even with his finest effort he was not going to be able to stretch the tour beyond ten minutes. "I think we're having tacos today."

It was an impulse the other guys would probably make him pay for for a long time. They never invited anybody for the hot lunches and suppers they took turns cooking.

"Oh, tacos," Amber breathed.

"*Tacos,*" Tucker bellowed so loudly that even Sadie laughed. A ghost of her old laugh was in there.

But she answered quickly. "We can't. I'm sorry, but we just can't."

"Please, Auntie Angel. Please."

"*Tacos,*" Tucker bellowed again.

"I didn't bring any formula for the baby," she said, casting a glance his way. The baby was still sleeping like a rock.

And then a loud alarm started to go off over them. The children covered their ears as the loud *wah wah wah* echoed through the building, and men began to run from everywhere.

The baby woke with a screech, and Michael leaned very close to Sadie as she scooped him up from the stroller. "Gives a whole new meaning to 'saved by the bell,' doesn't it?"

He bent low, and pried Tucker's hand away from his ear long enough to say something to him.

And then he spun away from them and joined his colleagues. In a blink they had shrugged into the equipment that waited for them beside the truck. In another blink the fire-hall doors were open and the truck was gone, siren growing fainter as it moved away.

"That was wonderful." Amber sighed.

"Tacos," Tucker said happily.

"Not today, I'm afraid," Sadie said with abject relief. A few more minutes with Michael and she had an awful feeling she would've split wide open, and out of the shell would have hoped the Sadie she used to be—gum cracking, hair dyed brassy blond. The works.

"Could we come back and have lunch sometime?" Amber asked enthusiastically.

"No," Sadie said, a little more sharply than she intended. She had not expected to see Michael, and so she had not been in the least prepared for their encounter.

She had not been prepared for her naked awareness of him. She had not been prepared for how big and handsome he had looked in the navy blue uniform shirt, and the matching trousers.

She had not been prepared for his gentle patience with the children, for the sense of humor that had coaxed Amber the Grim to laugh again and again.

She had not been prepared for the pure masculine appreciation that lit golden fires in his eyes when he had looked at her.

She had certainly not been prepared for the strength of his hand when he had shaken hers, nor for the shiver of shocked appreciation that his touch caused to race down her spine and curl in the pit of her tummy like a passionately purring cat.

She had put on that stupid ring this morning on an impulse, thinking a few thousand dollars' worth of diamonds on her finger would give her an air of confidence and panache.

Instead, she found she had least of all been prepared to answer questions about her engagement.

Nearly engagement.

When was she going to *officially* fall for Kevin? She felt angry at Michael for even making her wonder such a silly thing. So what if it wasn't firecrackers and shaken-up soda she felt for him? There were other things in life.

Like security.

Like being someone.

Walking home, she took off the ring and put it in her pocket. Her hand felt better without it on.

When they got home she was astonished when Tucker went directly to the kitchen table and sat down.

"Lunch," he demanded.

"No tacos, Tucker," Sadie told him. "I don't have the ingredients." Not to mention she didn't know how to make them, though she was sure it would be easy enough to find out.

Tucker surprised her by being unperturbed by her announcement of no tacos.

With great appetite, he ate the humble offering she set before him for lunch, listening with avid interest as Amber relived the fire hall in every minute detail.

"Want to go outside?" Amber asked him hopefully after lunch. "We could play in the leaves."

"Leaves," he echoed approvingly, and followed his sister out the door.

Moments later, as Sadie fed the baby, she could hear the sounds of their delighted shrieks coming in the window.

Tucker out from under the bed, and Amber happy.

And somehow she had Michael O'Bryan to thank for all this and resented it deeply.

But not as deeply as she was going to.

CARA COLTER   45

                                  * * *

The doorbell rang about four-thirty, just as Sadie was
beginning her nightly ritual of panicking about what to
cook for dinner. Tucker had remained out from underneath
the bed, and was now glued to the TV set yelling encour-
agement at his favorite cartoon characters.

Sadie was not a good cook, and cooking held no enjoyment for her. In Seattle she ate out quite a lot, and she had
planned to do the same thing here. Tucker under the bed
had put a stop to that plan.

Plus, with nearly a week of substitute parenting under
her belt she now knew that in reality taking three small
children out to a restaurant would probably be far more
difficult than staying home with them.

Still, the pleasure of macaroni and cheese and tinned
noodles in various unlikely shapes was wearing a little thin.
She was going to have to get a cookbook.

She went to the door. It had one of those lovely frosted
glass ovals in it, and she peered out, her hard-learned big-
city suspicion not yet having succumbed to Sleepy Grove's
small town charm.

Gasping, she flung herself against the wall.

She was not opening the door to him. And that was *official.*

"Who is it, Auntie Angel?" Amber padded out of the
living room, and gave Sadie an astonished look. "What are
you doing?"

Sadie unglued herself from the wall. "Uh, dusting the
wallpaper."

"With your fanny?" Amber went up to the door. She
looked out and a grin split her face. Without hesitating she
flung open the door. "Hi, Michael! Tucker said you were
coming, but I didn't believe him for sure. Sometimes he's
kind of a baby."

Sadie slid away from the wall. "Oh, it's you," she said,

as if she was completely surprised and his unexpected presence had not sent her scuttling for cover.

"I brought the kids some leftover tacos. I told Tuck I would on the condition he stayed out from underneath the bed."

Tucker had heard the voice and came out of the living room. His eyes brightened when he saw Michael.

"Tacos?" he asked hopefully.

"Did you keep your end of the bargain, my man? Did you stay out from underneath the bed?"

Tucker nodded solemnly, his eyes fastened on the large brown paper bag in Michael's hands.

"Then here you are. Tacos."

"Ooohh," Tucker breathed with such ecstatic appreciation that even Sadie had to smile.

"I take it he's a little tired of my cooking," she said.

"Me, too," Amber said with childish directness. "Are you going to eat with us, Michael?"

Sadie felt her mouth fall open and a tide of heat flash up her cheeks.

Michael's eyes were on her, amused, and faintly derisive. He looked meaningfully at her hand, and then his eyes widened mockingly at her naked ring finger.

"I was doing dishes!" she said.

"Hey, look, it's not as if it's *official,* anyway."

From their brief encounter all those years ago, she knew he had enough ego for ten men. How could he not? Every single woman they had encountered had fawned over him shamelessly. It wouldn't hurt to have it pricked. Michael O'Bryan could be brought down a peg or two.

"Tonight's not convenient," she said stiffly.

That didn't feel nearly as good as she thought it would. In fact, she was wrestling a demon inside her that wanted nothing more than to stand back from that door and offer to share his own tacos with him.

"I had tacos for lunch, anyway." He was smiling as if he *knew* all about that demon.

"Well, thanks," Amber said, shooting her aunt a dirty look.

"Yes, thanks," Sadie said, and found the bag, warm and aromatic, shoved into her hands.

"Oh," he said, "I wanted to give you this, too." He pulled a piece of paper from his shirt pocket and handed it to her.

She juggled the bag and took the slip of paper warily.

MICHAEL, it said in bold black letters, followed by his phone number.

She stared at him in astonishment. He didn't really think she was going to phone him, did he? Her feeling of wanting to share a taco with him vanished, and was replaced by something so white-hot, it surprised her. Fury. Fury at the pure unadulterated ego of the man.

She'd told him she was engaged. Almost.

"Sometimes you'd be surprised what can go wrong with these old places," he told her, apparently missing the killing light in her eyes. "And it always happens in the middle of the night when all you can get is the plumber's answering machine."

He was grinning, now, as if he was well aware she had misinterpreted that phone number entirely.

"Last year," he continued amiably, "it was my furnace. In the middle of the night, coldest night of the year. If you have an emergency like that, don't hesitate to call me."

She searched his face for hidden messages. For middle-of-the-night innuendo that she could get properly worked up about.

There was none that she could detect.

"Thank you," she managed to choke out.

"You look very pretty when you blush," he said with a wink, and then turned on his heel and was gone.

She stared at him making his way down the walk. He turned and gave her a casual wave just as if he knew she would be there, completely mesmerized by how good his backside looked in those uniform pants.

She slammed the door so hard, the frosted glass rattled in the frame.

"Oh, Auntie Angel—" Amber sighed "—he thinks you're pretty."

"He does not. He says that to all the girls."

"How do you know?"

"I just know."

"He didn't say it to me," Amber pointed out.

"I have a man in my life, Amber, so it doesn't matter if he thinks I'm pretty or not."

"You mean Kevin?"

"How do you know?"

"I heard my dad talk about him after you all went for lunch that day in Seattle. He told Mommy your boyfriend was a pom-pom ass. What does that mean?"

"Ass is a word little girls don't use."

"Well, I didn't really use it, I just *repeated* what my daddy said. I know what pom-poms are, and I know what the other word is, too, because sometimes my dad tells my mom she has a nice one, but I don't understand how it goes together."

"Ass sometimes means donkey," Sadie said. Mickey didn't like Kevin?

"So your boyfriend's a pom-pom donkey?"

She should have been offended. But somehow she couldn't be. She could just picture Kevin's reserved face if she called him a pom-pom donkey. She started to laugh.

"Is your boyfriend a pom-pom donkey?" Amber insisted.

Sadie howled. "It's not official yet," she finally managed to choke out to her puzzled niece. "Now go finish watching cartoons. I'll call you when the tacos are heated up."

Still chortling, she went into the kitchen and set the bag down on the table. Then, feeling just a touch guilty about her disloyalty to Kevin, she very deliberately crunched up the piece of paper with Michael's phone number on it and threw it in the garbage.

It felt so good to do that, that she fished it out, and straightened it, all for the satisfaction of crumpling it once more and throwing it again on top of old potato peelings.

But the third time she took it out, she found herself straightening the crumples, and staring at the bold strokes with which he had written his name.

Could he be right? Things did go wrong with these old houses with distressing regularity. The plumbing, the wiring, the heating.

It would be nice to know she had someone to call in case of an emergency. Of course, she could call Hawk Adams, but he and Kate lived across town. Michael O'Bryan lived so close and could get there in the blink of an eye.

It was childish to throw out the number. She'd put it in the kitchen drawer in case of emergency.

After all, she'd already had her emergency for this year. She doubted there would be another for a long time.

Every time she opened this drawer she could see that number and congratulate herself on not having used it. The truth was, the furnace could break down, and hell could freeze over, and she wasn't going to use the number.

She was going to keep it.

But not use it. It was too much to hope that he might sit by his phone waiting for it to ring.

His phone probably rang all the time. But it wouldn't be her at the other end of the line needing his big strong self to help her out of a pinch.

That was a vow.

But she should have known by now. When a McGee made a vow, things almost invariably went wrong.

Chapter Three

"Auntie Angel, wakie."

Sadie blinked open her eyes to see Tucker's face very close to hers. He was dressed in fluffy, blue footed sleepers, and he was shaking her shoulder vigorously.

Fire was her first thought. She sat up and sniffed the air. She noticed, somewhat blearily, that it was only just dawn, the guest room where she slept bathed in watery pastel shades.

Tucker had taken to pulling on her arm with his free arm. With his other he had a headlock around his bunny, Snappy.

Her waking mind was now telling her that fire was out of the question. There was no smoke and no smell of smoke. But that didn't mean the basement wasn't at this moment filling slowly with water, or that a burglar wasn't stuck upside down in their chimney.

Tucker's gray eyes were huge in their distress, and his chubby bottom lip was quivering.

She shoved back the thick patchwork quilt and gave in

to Tucker's none-too-gentle urging to follow him. He led
her over to her window and pointed.

"Monster," he said, his voice squeaky with near panic.

She felt herself relax, but still obediently squinted out in
the direction of his finger. The yard was quiet in the early-
morning light. The maple was still magnificent in its red-
and-gold finery.

She had left the window open a crack, and the air stirred
the lace curtain, fresh and autumn scented.

She sighed with something like contentment. Seattle was
beautiful, too. But it had a lively kind of beauty, a surging
energy. And her apartment looked out at another apartment,
and a busy street. The air smelled of car exhaust and sometimes of the sea, but she had missed the tangy scent of
leaves on damp grass, and wood smoke in early-morning
air.

"Monster," Tucker repeated urgently.

Sadie crouched beside him and put a reassuring arm
around his sturdy shoulders. "Auntie Angel will protect
you from monsters," she told him, already thinking of
crawling back in between the warm welcome of her flannel
sheets.

"No!" he shrieked. He pulled out from under the weight
of her arm, dropped Snappy, took her head in his hands
and forced it back toward the window. "Monster!"

Dutifully, she returned her attention to the view out the
window, realizing he saw her as guilty of not taking his
monster seriously enough.

Amber padded in, rubbing one eye sleepily, dragging
behind her a huge teddy bear by his ear. "I heard Tucker
yelling. What's wrong?"

"Tucker says there's a monster in the yard."

"Really?" Amber asked eagerly, joining them at the
window. "Where, Tuck?"

This apparently was more like it. Tucker took Amber's hand and pointed back at the yard, jabbering unintelligibly.

"He says it's in the garden," Amber interpreted officiously. "In the corn."

Sadie obligingly studied the garden.

"I saw something move!" Amber said.

In a minute they were both going to work themselves into a frenzy, Sadie thought uneasily, and that would be the end of crawling back in between those warm flannel sheets.

Sadie realized she had to take firm control of the situation right now. "There is nothing in the gard— Oh, God!" Sure enough, the cornstalks, not yet cut down for the year, suddenly swayed violently. Even in the house they could hear the crunch and rattle of the dry, spiky leaves.

There was something in the garden! Something huge! Something hiding right behind the cornstalks.

"Monster?" Tucker asked her, turning wide fear-filled eyes toward her. He picked Snappy back up, tucked him under his arm and slurped nervously on his thumb.

"Of course not," Sadie said as evenly as she could, squinting at the now-still corn.

"Let's go see!" Amber suggested.

Sadie caught her firmly by the wrist as Amber spun away from the window, and tucked her in close to her side. "I don't think so."

The corn swayed again. Sadie caught the briefest glimpse of something, before the curtain of corn swayed closed.

Amber must have seen it, too, because she gasped.

"What was that, Auntie Angel?"

Sadie groped across the antique washstand beside her, feeling for the phone without taking her eyes off the window. She didn't know what it was, but she wasn't going out there to see, and she wasn't being held prisoner inside the house all day, either.

She could have thrown out that piece of paper with his phone number on it after all, because the number was emblazoned on her brain.

He answered on the second ring, his voice amazingly cheerful for—Sadie glanced at the clock—just after six in the morning.

"Michael, it's me," she whispered as if the beast in the garden might be alerted to her calling for help if she spoke too loudly. "Sadie. Your neighbor. Amber's aunt."

"I know who you are," he said dryly. "We shared an unforgettable afternoon together flying a kite. Remember?"

She did remember. Every detail. Vividly. His smile, and the ripple of his arms, and the gold flecks in his eyes. And a kite soaring on the wind, and the way the string felt tugging at her hands, and her breath coming so hard from laughing and running. For a moment he had given her a gift so precious. The childhood she had never had.

Shoot. It was early and her defenses were way down.

"I'm sorry to wake you," she said with stiff formality, not letting one little warm morsel of that memory into her voice.

"I was up," he said cheerfully.

For a sick moment she wondered if there was someone with him, and she strained to hear background noises, and then was ashamed of herself.

"I don't want to bother you, but there seems to be something in the garden. It's scaring the children." Of course her own heart was beating more wildly by the second, and the deep growl of his voice seemed to have as much to do with it as the unidentified creature crashing around in the corn.

"Something in the garden? Like what?"

He had a damnably sexy voice, deep and sure.

"I don't know. It's hiding in the corn, but I'm sure it's a large animal of some kind."

Considering it was a state of emergency she really shouldn't be wondering what he thought of *her* voice. But she was.

"You better stay in the house," he said, his calm in no way disguising the fact he had not just made a suggestion, but given an order. "It may be only a deer, but there have been several reports of a black bear foraging in gardens out this way."

"A bear," she repeated weakly, gluing her gaze on the corn.

"A bear!" Amber said with undisguised delight.

The corn parted, and a huge hairy head appeared for a moment, and then disappeared.

"It's not a bear," Sadie whispered to Michael. "And it's not a deer, either."

"You saw it?"

"Just now. Just for a second. I think it's some sort of pig. With long hair."

There was a prolonged pause.

"A pig?" Michael finally asked.

"Only bigger. With piggier eyes than a pig."

She heard something suspiciously like a snort. "Are you laughing?"

"No. I swear, I'm not laughing."

She knew he was laughing. She could picture his white teeth and the flash of gold in his eyes.

It was really much too early for this type of exposure to him.

"Don't come out of the house," he ordered again. "I'll be right there."

As they watched for another glimpse of the elusive shape

in the corn, Michael appeared suddenly from the corner of
the house.

He had come more quickly than she thought was possible. He must have already been dressed. Sadie noticed with
a shudder that he had a rifle slung over his shoulder.

Amber gasped when she saw it, and Tucker clapped his
hand over his mouth.

All three of them held their breaths as Michael made his
way steadily across the backyard toward the garden patch.
The cornstalks swayed suddenly, noisily, and he stopped
and unslung the rifle from his shoulder.

Sadie wanted to yell at him not to go any farther. They
could call the police. They could call the fire department.
But he was already stepping into the corn and it was too
late.

Once upon a time she would have thought death in a
corn patch by an unknown ogre would have been a fitting
end for Michael O'Bryan. When she'd returned to Spokane
and he'd *obeyed* her and not phoned. Never again shown
up at her apartment door with a smile on his face and a
kite tucked under his arm.

When exactly had she changed her mind?

Long before this morning, actually. When Kate had
phoned. Four years ago? And told her Michael had been
badly hurt in a high-speed chase.

She had never told Kate how she felt about Michael, and
yet Kate, so intuitive, seemed to know.

"Sadie," she'd said, ever so gently. "They're not sure
if he's going to make it."

He'd been brought to a hospital in Spokane, and nothing
could have stopped Sadie from going to him. Even if she
had ordered herself not to go, her feet would have gone
anyway. If she had chained herself to her sofa, she would

have chewed through the chains with her own teeth and gone to him.

So she'd gone. She'd lied with amazing ease to the nurse, and been allowed into his room.

He was unconscious. He was burned badly. She couldn't even touch him.

It didn't matter. She sat through the night, being with him. Talking to him about flying kites, and about dreams, about where she had been and about where she was going.

In the long darkness of that night she had told herself that if he lived, she wouldn't ever leave him again.

But morning had brought his current girlfriend, a tall gorgeous redhead.

"Who are you?" she'd demanded.

What could Sadie say? *The one who loves him best of all* came to her heart but not her lips.

"Just an old friend," she'd murmured. She'd still been in college, and she was suddenly aware of her faded jeans, and her jean jacket with the elbow out.

"Well, let's keep it that way, shall we?" the redhead had said, her eyes catlike slits.

Though Sadie kept track of his progress in ways that were creative and probably illegal, she didn't go back, respecting the fact he had gone on to build a life that didn't include her.

And now, here he was, this same man, defying death again, about to be ripped to shreds by a wild piggie-eyed creature of an unknown species, and here she was, facing the very same feelings deep inside herself.

Of somehow having missed what was most important of all.

He seemed to have been gone from sight a long time. Amber closed her eyes and put her hands over her ears.

Tuck buried his head in Sadie's shoulder. Sadie held her breath waiting for the awful report of the rifle.

The corn swayed violently once more, and then parted as Michael stepped out of the garden and onto the grass.

She gasped in astonishment. Amber opened her fingers and looked out between them. Tucker turned his head ever so slightly so he could see.

Both the children squealed with delighted surprise and were up and racing for the door in the blink of an eye. Even Snappy lay abandoned facedown on her bedroom floor.

Sadie looked through the window and shook her head. Not a bear, and not a pig, either, though she could see why she'd been fooled.

Standing in the yard with Michael O'Bryan was a shaggy brown-and-white pony, the pony's shoulder no higher than Michael's waist. She'd been absolutely right about one thing.

That pony had piggy eyes.

As she watched, the children stampeded across the yard. Amber threw her arms around the pony's neck and kissed him right on the tip of his pink nose as if she were greeting a long-lost relation. Tucker locked his pudgy arms around the pony's knee and buried his face in the dirty fur.

Michael laughed, and it was a sound as rich as the morning. For a moment, watching them, Sadie felt an ache of bittersweet wanting.

Abruptly she left her perch by the window. She was going to have to go out, no doubt about that. But damned if he was going to see her in her baggy-bottomed pajamas again.

She pulled on a pair of freshly laundered jeans and a sweater that did slightly more for her modest curves than her flannel shirt had done. She did her best to calm the spikes in her hair, and briefly allowed herself to mourn the fact that makeup was absolutely out. If she put on makeup at this hour of the morning, he was bound to guess it wasn't to impress the pony.

She hesitated, and then dug deep into the pocket of the jacket she'd been wearing yesterday and extricated the ring. She frowned at it, then jammed it on her finger.

By the time she got outside, he'd found a string somewhere and attached it to a very worn and faded red halter. He was leading the pony around the yard with Amber and Tucker on board.

"Can we keep him, Auntie Angel?" Amber called almost before Sadie was off the bottom steps.

She walked toward them. Amber hadn't looked this flushed with happiness in a long, long time. Not even the fire hall had done this.

But of course, keeping the pony was out of the question.

"I'm afraid we can't keep him," she said, trying not to be so frightfully aware of Michael O'Bryan.

He was wearing jeans today, faded nearly white, that hugged the perfect curve of his rear and the hard muscle of his legs. He had on a hooded navy blue pullover with a police department emblem on it. His hair was wet, and the faint smell of soap tickled her nostrils. He must have just gotten out of the shower, and Michael O'Bryan in the shower was one direction she could not let her wayward mind journey in.

"That pony belongs to someone," she said, shifting her attention quickly to the animal.

Close up, it was evident the animal was in a pathetic condition. His shaggy coat was nearly an inch long in places, and matted with dirt and burrs. His ribs stuck out. His white mane and tail were so tangled and full of burrs, it seemed it would take days of patient work to get him clean. The halter was worn nearly right through, and had rubbed the hair right off his nose in places. He had unfortunately small eyes, and seemed to be regarding Sadie out of the corner of one of them with wary weariness.

She made the mistake of reaching out and touching him on his shoulder. His fur was warm and surprisingly soft, and she felt an unwanted stab of liking for him.

"What are we going to do with him?" she wondered out loud.

"Keep him," Amber and Tucker howled together.

Sadie stared at them in dismay, and then felt Michael watching her his eyes lit with amusement or sympathy, she couldn't tell which.

"Hey, kids," he said lifting them down from the pony's back, "go and see if you can find a bucket to put some water in for him. He's probably thirsty."

Amber and Tucker showed amazing enthusiasm for this small responsibility and took off at a dead run.

"I guess we'll have to call the SPCA," Sadie decided, then wondered what this "we" stuff was.

He laughed, and she scowled at him. Did he have to have such a nice laugh? And such a nice voice? And such nice eyes? Did he have to be so damnably perfect? She bet if he took off his shoes, he'd even have those kind of toes that went down in a perfect progression, instead of having his second toe sticking up higher like the rest of the world.

"We don't have an SPCA here. You're not used to small towns anymore, are you?"

Not anymore. Of course, she'd grown up here, but hers was the kind of family more likely to be placing urgent calls to AA than the SPCA.

"I live in Seattle," she said, giving away none of her history.

"I heard."

Did that mean he had asked someone specifically about her, or only that he'd heard it, by chance, sometime in his travels? She might wear her hair differently and her makeup differently, but somewhere inside her lurked that vulnerable girl who had wanted so badly for things to work out between them.

"A big-city girl now," he said with a wry shake of his head.

"Meaning?" she asked him more sharply than she meant to.

"Meaning you aren't going to know the first thing about the care and keep of a small homeless pony."

But they both knew that wasn't what he had meant. He'd been thinking of the small town girl she used to be. Naive, somehow, under that protective shell she'd created around herself. Innocent, despite all her attempts to act worldly.

"That's right. I don't know anything about ponies. That's why we can't keep him." There was that "we" again. Of course, she meant herself and Amber and Tucker and Tyler. Not herself and Michael O'Bryan. Somehow she knew she'd botch it up terribly if she tried to explain it, though.

"Luckily for you I know the rudiments of pony care."

"I said we can't keep him," she said, sending him a warning look.

"Well, what do you propose to do? Just let him go? Walk out to the street with him and slap him on the rump? Hope he finds his way to a different person's garden?"

"Perhaps yours," she said stiffly, "since you know the rudiments of pony care."

"But I don't have a little garden shed, just like that one over there."

"I can't keep the pony!" she repeated, quite pleased

with herself that she was back in singular. "It's tough enough looking after two small children and a baby."

"Are you having a tough time?" he asked gently.

"It's just an adjustment," she said, resisting the gentleness of his tone, and the confidences it invited. Oh, to just be able to tell him about the misery of trying to get dinner done every night. "I'm not used to it yet."

"What are you used to?"

"I work for a public-relations firm in Seattle. I'm a marketing executive."

"Oh," he said. "A *career* woman from the big city. Baby-sitting must be quite the let-down for you."

"It is not!"

He was getting her mad again, and from the look on his face enjoying it thoroughly.

"I'm glad to be spending time with Amber and my nephews." She didn't add that she could have enjoyed it a little more without having to look after diapers and meals. "Besides, my company has some business down here I can look after at the same time."

Not that she had yet, but how capable that made her sound! Not only was she looking after three children, but she was going to do her job, too! Planning to do her job. Very soon.

"How is Samantha?" he asked, the concern in his voice very real.

"There's something wrong with her kidneys. It's beginning to look like a transplant is going to be the only solution. She's seeing some specialists right now."

"I hope it works out."

"Me, too," she said, but just talking about it had brought her fear and tension to the surface. She swiped quickly at an eye.

"You're handling a lot. I'm right across the street if you need anything."

She did not want his sympathy, that was for darn sure! "I just need you to help me get rid of the pony. I don't want the kids getting attached to him when they can't have him."

"You probably could keep him for a couple of days," he said quietly. "We'll put an ad in the newspaper, and on the radio."

Now he was speaking in plural, and he didn't have Amber and Tucker and Tyler to use for an excuse.

We, as in he and she, Sadie, in this together.

It caused a funny surging warmth in her that she most certainly did not want to feel.

"It would break their hearts if we kept him and then had to let him go."

"Maybe not. He looks like a pony somebody doesn't have the time for. They might be happy to have a couple of kids come visit him every now and then."

Sadie wasn't so sure. Anybody who'd let a pony get this run-down was probably no great lover of visiting children, either.

"How can we keep him even for a few days? We don't have a fence or a shelter."

"That garden shed over there is nearly empty. That would make an okay shelter. And I could knock up a fence that would hold him in."

She was aware of him looking down at her from his greater height, a smile on his face that would melt hearts a lot harder than hers.

She didn't want him here, building a fence and chatting with the children, and being *in* her life.

No, she realized, that was an absolute lie. She wanted him here very badly.

She wanted to hear his laughter and watch him kid with the children, and see his muscles gleaming with sweat under the warm autumn sun.

Still vulnerable to him, after all these years.

And now she was all grown-up and should know better.

Michael watched the play of emotions across her face. She was not as transparent as she once had been, but he could still read her pretty good.

She wanted him to stay, and didn't, too.

Which was nearly identical to how he was feeling himself. He didn't want to tangle with Sadie again. She wasn't staying here and he wasn't leaving. She'd become some kind of big-town girl, and he was still a small-town boy.

They hadn't had a hope before, and they certainly didn't have one now.

All the same, she'd been fun. And under some of that priss and polish he was willing to bet she still was. So why not have some harmless fun for a few days? A few laughs, and then say goodbye.

He was kidding himself. Life was never that simple. They'd had a few laughs last time, and that goodbye had hurt him for a good long while. He'd barely known her, and it had had that effect on him.

Build the pony pen, and then say goodbye and mean it.

"How long are you here for?" he asked her.

"Probably about ten days."

Ten days. Wasn't that about how long it had been last time? And a few of those days had been just long distance days, not face-to-face days.

Put that heart in armor, son, he instructed himself. This girl carries a sharpened spear.

Though you sure wouldn't know it to look at her. She was as soft looking as spring buttercups. Though, come to think of it, she hadn't always been. Her eyes had always been soft, leading him think that tough-girl image was mostly bravado.

More the fool him.

I'm never coming back here, she'd told him. Don't ever call me again, get it?

Get it. Yeah, he'd gotten it.

Still, she had changed. Once, something rustling in the yard would have had her out there with her baseball bat, yelling challenges at it.

Or would it? Was that just part of the bravado, too?

He sighed.

"Having second thoughts about the pony?" she asked him.

Second thoughts, all right. "Not about the pony," he said. "I'm going to need to organize some materials."

"Would you like me to provide the beer?" she said sweetly. Too sweetly. Like she *wanted* him to be the kind of guy who swilled beer every time he picked up a hammer, so she could hold him in disdain.

Which meant she was fighting something, too, despite the king-size rock on her finger that kept twisting around backward. That pony arriving in her yard had just flung them into the dangerous ground of a mutual attraction that had not dimmed much with time.

He tried to remember if he ever drank too much when they'd been together. He couldn't remember drinking at all. Being with her had been a heady enough experience, not to mention one that required a man keep his wits about him.

"I don't drink," he said.

"You don't?"

"No. Being a cop turned me right off it. It seemed like

ninety-five percent of what I dealt with was alcohol related.''

"I don't drink, either.'' She blushed suddenly, appealingly, as if realizing it sounded like she was trying to find things in common between them. ''Of course, you know what I come from.''

"Yeah.'' So, underneath that store-bought confidence, she still had the chip on her shoulder. As if the whole town watched her and judged where she came from. Waited for her to become just like her old man. It had never mattered to him. And it had never stopped mattering to her.

"I'll get my tools and some materials and be back in a while,'' he told her.

"Can I go with you?'' Amber asked, just returning with a not-very-full bucket of water.

"Me, too?'' Tucker asked.

Michael raised his eyebrows at Sadie. ''Can they?''

"You don't drink, and you like kids?''

"You don't have to say it like it's an indictment.''

"I just wondered where you store your wings when you're not wearing them.''

"Doesn't your boyfriend like kids?''

"I've never asked him.''

"What?'' It exploded out of him.

"Pom-pom Donkey,'' Amber crowed. ''That's what I'm going to call my pony.''

"It's not your pony, honey,'' Sadie told her, but she was looking daggers at him.

"I like that name,'' Michael told Amber, returning Sadie's look, plus a little. She was thinking of marrying a guy who might not like kids—hadn't even asked him. ''What do you guys talk about, anyway? Stocks? Fine points of the law?''

"What I talk to my fiancé about is none of your business."

"No kidding. Probably bore me near to death."

"It probably would," she agreed haughtily, insinuating he was some small-town hick.

"You told me once you wanted a dozen kids someday."

"I did?"

"Yeah, you did. You said you were going to teach them to fly kites and ride bicycles."

"I was seventeen, for heaven's sake! A dozen children is preposterous."

"Well, how many do you want?"

"I haven't thought about it! I'm just establishing my career at the moment."

He found himself wanting to take her shoulders and give them a good shake—shake the real Sadie out from her. Instead, he turned away. "I'll go get the stuff I need."

"Can we go with him?" Amber demanded.

"All right," she said. "You'll need to get dressed." A few moments later she watched Amber and Tuck scamper after Michael. "Two children," she yelled at his departing back. "Three at the most."

He didn't even turn back, but he reached down and picked up Tucker, placing him way up on his shoulder.

Sadie felt immediately mortified. Why did he make her behave like this?

She stomped into the house. There was nothing wrong with putting off the decision to have kids. She had decided a long time ago—right after it had dawned on her that Michael O'Bryan was *never* calling—that romantic entanglements and families and all that stuff had no place in the life of a woman who was going to be as dedicated to her career as she was.

The baby had not awakened yet when Sadie went into

the house. It seemed to her to be the first silence she had heard since signing on here.

How she'd enjoyed silence when she first got her apartment in Seattle. Or maybe silence was the wrong word. In the big city there was always sound, even in the dead of night. She'd enjoyed being alone. Her privacy. Her independence.

Now, after five minutes, she missed the noise and activity of the kids. Him and his stupid impertinent, personal questions!

She had the strangest feeling since coming back here to Sleepy Grove. As if that whole world she'd so carefully created for herself in Seattle was not real. Was not even there anymore now that she was here.

She went into the bathroom and carefully curled her hair so that it wouldn't look like it had been curled, and carefully applied makeup so that it wouldn't look like she had put on makeup.

After a while the baby woke up, and she gave him breakfast and listened to the truck pull into the yard, and the children leap out shrieking.

She could hear Amber jabbering away a mile a minute, and Michael's deep voice responding.

And she felt that funny ache, again. As if this was something she wanted for herself. A baby, children in the yard Saturday morning, a husband who was handsome and full of fun.

Not that Kevin wasn't handsome, though it would be a stretch to call him full of fun.

Sadie knew something suddenly about her life in Seattle that she didn't want to know.

She was busy. Her job was demanding and creative. She was successful. She had Kevin.

And she was lonely.

She bundled the baby up in his plaid logger's jacket and put on one herself. She carried him outside and watched his eyes widen at the sight of the pony.

Michael, who was digging fence posts, and sweating, grinned at her. Amber and Tucker were clearing out the garden shed.

"Michael bought us a brush for the pony," Amber squealed.

"Hay," Tucker added, now an authority on the care and keeping of small ponies.

She brought the baby over to the pony, who did not bother to lift his head from the hay he was munching with incredible speed. The baby grabbed a fistful of mane and blubbered wildly.

"What am I going to do when the owner comes?" Sadie asked miserably, watching the happy activity.

"Maybe he won't come," Michael said. "The pony looks abandoned."

"Nobody abandons a pony. It would be awful for the kids to even think that."

"Stranger things have happened."

"Yes." She had to agree, thinking of their few whirlwind days of romance all those years ago, and the fact they were now sharing each other's company in her brother's backyard. "I guess they have."

"The way I look at it," he said softly, "that little girl's heart was breaking. She needed something, and it came."

"A gift from heaven?" Sadie snorted cynically.

He just shrugged and smiled.

"It'll be worse when the pony goes."

He shrugged again. "The pony came when it was supposed to, I imagine it will go when it's right, too."

What had happened to him?

Her eyes drifted to the scars just visible along the neck-line of his T-shirt.

He caught her looking.

"I got them in a high-speed chase."

"I heard," she said.

His eyebrows went up, and she knew he was wondering if she had *heard* or if she had asked specifically about him.

"While I was in the hospital the first night, I dreamed you were with me. An angel calling me back to earth. A funny coincidence that your niece calls you Angel."

"Well, everybody knows that I'm not," she said uncomfortably, and turned quickly from his penetrating gaze to stroke the pony's matted fur.

"Do they?" he asked quietly, "Everybody?"

She rubbed the pony more vigorously. He was trying to say she had a chip on her shoulder. What would he know? He'd been born an O'Bryan, not a McGee.

Too quickly for her to stop it, the overlarge ring caught on a matted piece of fur and slid from her finger right into the hay the pony was gulping down.

"No!" she cried, juggling the baby to her other hip, and stooping for the ring just as the pony moved to that portion of hay and gulped it down greedily.

"What?" Michael asked.

"The pony ate my ring," she said with disbelief. She set the baby down on his padded rear and sifted through the hay, hoping it wasn't true. "He ate my ring!"

Michael chuckled.

"It's not funny!"

"Well, maybe it is just a little bit," he said, and now he was laughing quite hard.

"That ring is worth a fortune," she shouted. Not to mention it didn't even officially belong to her yet!

Then he really started to laugh. "Bad Pom-Pom Donkey," he gasped. "Bad horse."

"Amber told you where that name came from," Sadie said accusingly.

"Yes," he admitted, now doubled over, holding his stomach, the laughter coming out of him in ripples that held on the crisp autumn air, that made the sun seem even brighter than it had before.

She glared at him, not that he noticed. She glared at the pony, who chewed on contentedly. She glared at Amber who had come over to share the joke.

"What happened, Auntie Angel?"

"That thing—" she pointed at the pony "—ate my ring. And that one—" she pointed at Michael "—thinks it's funny."

"It is just a little bit funny, Auntie Angel," Amber told her solemnly. "Don't worry about your ring. It will come out the other end."

"The other end?" she said, hardly mollified.

Amber nodded solemnly. Out of the corner of her eye she could see Michael nodding, too, still doubled over with laughter, apparently this new fact renewing his mirth.

"I know," Amber informed her confidentially, "because once when I didn't mean to, I swallowed my mommy's ring. Know what? It came out ever so shiny."

Michael howled. "Amber gets to keep the pony until the ring reappears," he choked out, "and you, Sadie, get a free ring cleaning!"

Her lips twitched. Oh, she didn't want to laugh. Her shoulders began to shake. It would be very wrong to laugh. She could feel an explosive tightness in her chest.

The first peep came out. And then she was sitting on the ground, laughing until the tears came out her eyes, laughing until her sides hurt, laughing like she hadn't laughed since

a kite had danced with the wind far over her heard many
long years ago.

And then she saw the way Amber was laughing, too, and
looking at Michael, love, pure and simple, shining out her
eyes.

Healing.

The pony snuffled in his hay, and then passed wind with
such a long drawn-out bleat that they all broke up into gales
of laughter again.

It occurred to her he was right about the pony. It had
come here because it was supposed to.

And so had he.

Chapter Four

Michael wished she wouldn't have laughed like that. It reminded him too much of their history. The first time he'd seen her he'd known she wasn't his type. At all.

But the first time she'd laughed, he'd changed his mind. Completely.

She had a child's pure delight in her, the capability to still have wonder. He'd been enchanted by her laughter, that special sparkle that lit her eyes when she let go.

Then and now.

But best not to forget the cause of her laughter—the loss of the engagement ring meant nothing about the engagement. It was not an omen.

She was almost officially an engaged woman. She hated Sleepy Grove. *She'd dumped him.*

Strike three, you're out, he said mentally to her.

She had stopped laughing, and was now crawling right underneath the pony, sifting through hay, giving him a rather delectable view of jeans pulled taut over lovely curves.

"He might have spit it out," she said. "No pony in his right mind is going to *swallow* a ring."

"Sadie, get out from under there," he said, his own rising blood pressure adding an unintended snap to his voice. "Horses are not the most predictable of animals."

"I don't know if he qualifies as a horse," she panted, trying to move the pony's stubborn foot off a little clump of hay.

"He didn't spit it out. The ring is gone. Get out—"

"More like a cross between a pig and a Saint Bernard," she muttered, ignoring him.

The pony lifted up his foot casually, held it cooperatively in the air for a moment, and then set it down. Smack-dab on the middle of her hand.

As he sprang forward Michael swore that the pony had a slight gleam in his eye that said *Call me a pig, will you?*

The pony stood there mildly chewing, his hoof planted solidly, Sadie trying to get her hand out from under, her face gone suddenly white with pain, her silence astounding. Michael bent and gave the tuft of hair at the back of the hoof a heave.

"Hoof," he commanded.

The pony lifted his foot, and Sadie slid her hand out and rolled out from underneath him.

She sat, hunched over, her back to him, rocking silently back and forth.

"Let me see."

"Nooo."

She had her hand cradled against her tummy. He winced. Even just looking over her shoulder it was evident her hand was already swelling.

"Let me see," he said, squatting down beside her.

"No!" she said again.

It was then that he realized how close to tears she was.

It was then that he realized she didn't want to cry in front of him.

This was the Sadie he remembered—anxious to appear as tough as nails, unhurtable, keeping all her pain to herself. A long time ago, when she'd said, "Get it?" in that tough tone of voice, had she been hiding something then?

Not worth thinking about. Even if they could turn back time and choose a different scenario, it would have still ended. She'd been very young.

And though he wouldn't have admitted it at the time, especially as the newest member of Sleepy Grove's police force, he hadn't exactly been Mr. Maturity himself.

He sank to his knees beside her.

"Go away."

"No."

He took her arm and gently wrestled the hand from her. Gently he probed. Her delicate little hand was beginning to look like a prize ham.

"Sadie, you don't have to be strong, you know," he told her quietly.

"Shut up," she said with the faintest edge of hysteria in her voice.

"You can cry if you want to."

"I'm not going to...cry." But she was, the tears starting slowly, and then flowing in rapid succession down her cheeks.

He realized she must have put on eye makeup this morning. Habit? Or for his benefit?

The sudden soft spot he felt for her was irresistible. He gathered her close to him and wiped the running makeup off with his sleeve. Slow, warm awareness seeped into him, awareness of the sweetness of her curves, the smell of her hair, the dampness of her tears. He resisted the sudden strong impulse to brush a kiss against the soft curve of her cheek.

He'd held many women, and some a great deal more passionately than this. So why was he aware of her as he had never been aware of any other woman?

Aware of her shape, and softness and aroma. Aware of the way she fit against him, and the silk of her skin pressed into his. So aware, he was tingling.

It was a good thing he was not even pretending to be administering first aid.

"It really hurts, huh?" he said to her. A very good thing. She howled.

It was a wonderful sound, so real and raw, it sent shivers up and down his spine. Completely gone was that polished mask that she had become so proficient at wearing.

Amber and Tucker appeared at his side and watched, wide-eyed and silent.

"The pony stepped on Auntie Angel's hand," Michael explained. "We're going to have to take her to the hospital."

"No," Sadie sobbed, "no hospital. I'll be fine. I'll—"

He held up her hand for her to see.

"Oh," she wailed. "I hate this town. First the fire, then my ring, now this. Don't you understand I'm not meant to be here?"

He was not sure if that's what he understood at all. When he'd had his accident at first he'd been filled with feelings of "why did this happen to me?" But later, maybe even only in the last few months, he'd seen something else. He was *happy* building fire trucks and renovating houses, in a way he never had been when he worked on the police department. He couldn't wait to tackle the old fire hall as his next, and his biggest renovation project.

He had never been a born policeman, like Hawk Adams.

The police uniform attracted women, which at one point he'd found very interesting. But the job itself he'd found ninety-nine percent boring, one percent exciting. And that one percent was going to be causing him an aching back for the rest of his life. It hardly seemed fair.

No more fair than having this beautiful woman in his arms when the farthest thing from her mind was kissing him.

Even so, maybe this small accident of Sadie's wasn't about bad luck at all.

He'd sworn he was building a fence for the pony and then clearing out of her life.

He looked at those three kids. He was pretty sure her hand was broken. How did one change a diaper with a broken hand? He wasn't actually all that sure how you did it with two good hands.

But it seemed to him fate had just deigned that he find out. Because beyond diapers, those three babies were going to need baths and meals and a lot of other things he had never even paused to think about before. Sadie was going to need his help.

And from the way her sobbing just intensified, she'd probably just figured that out, too.

She sat in the car beside him, her head lolling back, the pain in her hand throbbing so badly, it seemed to be moving right up her arm and into her shoulder.

He'd looked after everything with such calm. The pony tethered close to the hay, the kids organized and belted into the back seat of Sam and Mickey's minivan, her hand immobilized in a rough splint.

A very capable kind of guy she thought. It made her want to cry again. Because she was looking about the farthest thing from capable in the whole world.

The fire department called out, the ring lost and now a trip to the emergency ward.

It was making her look helpless, needy, clingy even, if the way she'd held on to him a few moments ago was any indicator. If there was one thing she despised it was a helpless, needy, clingy woman.

And knowing how much she despised that was the only thing that had finally made her let go of him. Otherwise she'd still be there sitting on the lawn, nestled into his lap, the comforting heat of his skin coming up through his shirt taking her pain away, making her into something she wasn't. The kind of woman that had to be pried away from a man with a crowbar.

"I hate this town," she muttered darkly to herself.

"I wish you'd quit saying that," he said. "Sleepy Grove has not become imbued with an evil spirit whose only purpose is to get Sadie McGee."

"How about embarrass me?" she asked him through clenched teeth. "Humiliate me? Make me look, and feel, like an accident looking for a place to happen."

He rolled his eyes and concentrated on the road. He was driving very fast, and with extreme competence.

His competence in every situation could become a real source of irritation, she told herself. Particularly if she was going to be on a real klutzy streak.

"Hurt, Auntie Angel?" Tuck called from the back seat.

"Not as bad," she lied, touched by his concern for her. They had come a long way since his sojourn under the bed.

In a few minutes, Michael pulled up in front of the emergency door at the hospital.

"Really," she said, "just park in the lot and I'll walk."

Michael rolled his eyes again, got out of his side and came over to hers, leaning across her to help her with the seat belt.

There was no point arguing she could do it herself. She already knew from the trip here that she could not. She had not realized before that doing up seat belts was a two-hand job.

He leaned over her. He smelled so good. His body was hard and uncompromising. His hair brushed her cheek, and she knew pain was weakening her, because she fought a ridiculous desire to kiss his cheek while he was so close.

Having released her, he gathered up the baby and herded the other two in front of him, managing to get her in the door.

"Grandpa," Amber yelled.

The tall, distinguished man in the white jacket turned and smiled at Amber.

Did it have to be Dr. Height? Sadie wondered grimly. This was what small towns were like. Everybody knew everybody. You always ran into the people you least wanted to see.

You caught your house on fire, your old beau turned up to put out the flame. Your hand got squashed by a pony, your brother's snobbish father-in-law was right there to look down his long straight nose at you.

When Mickey and Sam had first discovered each other, Dr. Height had disliked Mickey just because he didn't have the right pedigree. He'd forbidden Sam to see him. When Sam had run away to be with Mickey, the Heights had sent the police after her, as if loving a McGee were a criminal activity. It was all water under the bridge now, but Sadie had trouble forgiving and forgetting even if no one else seemed to.

Mickey and Sam had long since repaired the relationship with the Heights. Mickey, her renegade brother, actually golfed with his father-in-law. Mickey thought it was funny that his ragged jean jacket had been banned from the doctor's golf course.

Had his tremendous success as an artist made him acceptable to his in-laws? Or his ability to produce heart-meltingly cute grandchildren?

"Sadie," Dr. Height said kindly, coming over. She was surprised he remembered her name, and even more surprised by the genuine kindness in his voice. "What's happened?"

He gave Tuck a little chuck on the chin, and smiled at Tyler.

She held up her hand.

"That looks nasty," he said, taking her hand and looking at it. "How on earth did you do that?"

"A pony stepped on it. A fat pony."

He laughed. "It does hurt less when it's a skinny pony, I should think."

I should think. Shall we have tea now? She mocked his accent in her mind, even though she knew it was unfair and unkind.

The Heights had phoned her her first night on the job and offered their assistance, invited her for dinner.

She had politely but firmly refused. She had never been in their home, which she had cynically referred to as "the posh palace" when she was a teenager. She wasn't about to put herself in a position in which she'd have to worry about which fork to use, even though she'd become quite adept at forks since dating Kevin.

Now seeing the compassion in the doctor's face as he bent over her hand, she felt a stab of doubt. Would he even care what fork she used? Maybe *she* was the one caring about things that didn't matter.

Was Sleepy Grove really the way she thought it was, or had her own perception twisted it into something else?

"Michael, will you be okay with the kids while I look after Sadie, or should I call their grandma and ask her to come?"

"I'll be fine," he said. "Kindergarten ex-cop."

Even though her hand hurt like a hippo had stood on it instead of a midget horse, Sadie laughed.

Michael grinned back.

Beautiful teeth, she thought. Beautiful smile. It lit up his whole face, all the way to his eyes. He looked so fine with the baby in his arms, Tucker attached to one knee, Amber skipping around him.

He looked like...a daddy. Like a really good daddy. Calm and patient, full of laughter.

She closed her eyes when a fresh wave of pain struck her, only this time it wasn't being caused by her hand.

Someday he was going to be a daddy. Probably someday soon. He was getting to be that age when men settle down.

"Oh, hi, Michael."

A nurse, tall and dark and impossibly slender, with a nauseating baby voice, had just appeared. Of course, Sadie might not have thought her voice was so nauseating if it hadn't been dripping sugar at Michael.

"Hi, Wenda," he said casually. "How are you?"

Of course they'd know each other, Sadie thought. Policemen, firemen, nurses, always knew each other. And ended up married to each other, too.

"What a beautiful baby," Wenda cooed, going up to Michael and ignoring the patient all together. "He's one of Mickey's, I'll bet. I'd recognize a McGee anywhere."

Then try behind you and a little to the left, the other McGee thought with a savage lack of humor.

Again she was struck by that sense of everyone knowing everyone else. She had hated that when she was growing up here.

"Wenda, we're going to need an X ray on this hand," Dr. Height told the nurse. "And I'll need you to take Sadie's medical history. I'll see you in a minute in X ray, Sadie." He walked away.

Wenda turned most reluctantly from Michael. She looked at Sadie, then back to Michael and then at Sadie again.

"Are you together?"

"Yes," Michael said.

"No," Sadie said.

They glared at each other.

"Since we arrived in the same car, and are sharing responsibility for the same brood, wouldn't you say were together?" Michael pressed.

Sadie felt fire move up her cheeks. She hadn't thought of it like that. She'd thought of it like together *together*. A couple together. Forever. Stupid. The pain in her hand was affecting her brain, that was what.

"Together," she conceded. "Temporarily."

Obviously that was what the pretty nurse wanted to hear. She actually batted a thick set of lashes at Michael.

"I'm going to take the kids for breakfast," Michael informed Sadie, an edge of ice to his tone. If he had noticed the eyelash Olympics, he didn't show it. "I'll come back for you in—" He glanced at the nurse.

"Oh, not for at least an hour, probably more like two." The nurse disengaged herself from Michael with the same apparent reluctance that Sadie had recognized in herself and despised only minutes earlier, and took up her post behind the counter. "Your name?"

"Sadie *McGee*." The ones you recognize anywhere. Out of the corner of her eye, she could see Michael heading out the door. "Michael?"

He paused.

"I'm sorry. I mean, thank you. For being there for me."

He regarded her intently for a moment, then shook his head in that universal gesture of men that meant women completely baffled them.

It was nearly three hours later that Dr. Height came out to talk to Michael. Tucker and Amber were happily building a fort out of the coffee table and magazines. The baby was cheerfully incarcerated within the flimsy walls of the waiting area, though the odor of a diaper badly in need of changing had long since managed to escape.

"I'll release her to you in a minute," Dr. Height told Michael, who was pacing restlessly, the awful vinyl waiting room chairs murder on his back.

"There's a broken bone in her hand," Dr. Height informed him. "I've put it in a cast and given her something for the pain. You'll find her a little woozy. My concern is how she is going to manage. She didn't want me to call my wife, and I understand her reluctance, but she can't be on her own for tonight, at least, and after that with the three kids—" He glanced at them affectionately. "They're good kids, but a handful, even for someone with two hands."

Michael thought of Sadie, with that little chip on her shoulder, having to relinquish control of the kids to the Heights. She would feel like a terrible failure. Her illogical sense of Sleepy Grove being bad luck for her would be irrevocably sealed.

She would probably leave here and never come back. She'd made that vow once and broken it. He was willing to bet if she ever made it again they could cast it in cement and steel.

And for some reason, he wasn't ready for that to happen, even being fully aware she was spoken for. Almost officially.

"Maybe I should call her parents," Dr. Height suggested.

"No," Michael said vehemently.

"That's what I thought," Dr. Height said with a sigh.

"I'll look after it."

Dr. Height looked at him quizzically.

"I live right across the street," he said hastily.

"It's going to be a full-time job for a little while."

"I'm not doing anything better right now. I'm waiting for the town to start hearing proposals on the fire-hall property before I'll be really busy again."

"I'll look forward to seeing your proposal," Dr. Height said. He was a member of the town council. "The restoration you did on the old Barnaby place was delightful. One of the best I've seen. Didn't it get written up in *Heritage?*"

"It did," Michael said, with an effort at modesty, though he'd been thrilled with the write-up.

"I understand, aside from Mrs. Tuttleby's proposal for a pet cemetery at that location, a large out-of-town company will be putting in a proposal on that property, as well."

Michael felt jolted. It had never occurred to him that *his* proposal wouldn't get the go-ahead. He recovered quickly. A little competition was probably a good thing. It kept everybody honest and trying their hardest.

"A big out-of-town company?" Michael asked. "I can't help but wonder what they'd want with Sleepy Grove."

The doctor smiled. "I imagine our money is as green as anyone else's. Now, I'm going to give you this prescription to have filled. It's for painkillers. She may need them over the next few days. And I'll call Betty. I know Sadie is rather fiercely independent, but perhaps she won't regard a casserole and some baking as intruding too much on her territory."

The old doc was smart and sensitive, Michael realized.

He'd come a long way from the man who had been so violently opposed to Mickey and Samantha's union.

"I don't hold it against Sadie," the doctor continued quietly. "I was wrong about her brother. Stubbornly, stupidly wrong. I can tell Sadie's a woman of strong loyalties. It will be quite some time before she forgives me my error in judgment."

Michael knew Sadie well enough to know the doctor's judgment of her brother would have been taken personally, an indictment not just against Mickey but against herself, as well.

"I just finished telling Sadie this," the doctor continued. "The joy that young man has given my daughter is beyond measure. The way he's stood beside her through thick and thin gives new meaning to the word *devotion*. I'm deeply ashamed that I tried to stop a love like that from happening...especially now when I see Sam's time here might be..." His voice cracked. "I deserve Sadie's contempt."

"No, you don't," Michael told him. "We all make mistakes. You rectified yours. Samantha is one of the happiest women I've ever seen. Even sick, she positively glows. If you had made her choose between her husband and you, she could have never known that kind of happiness, but you didn't. As for Sadie, she's scared to death of not measuring up, and she's even more scared of anyone ever knowing that she's scared of anything. Don't mistake that for contempt."

"You know her quite well," the doctor said, clearing his throat, a little twinkle appearing in his eye.

"Not as well as I'm going to," Michael said.

"That's true," the doctor agreed.

Sadie came out, walking on a drunken tilt. Despite her hand neatly encased in white, and her arm tightly trussed in a sling, she managed to shove Wenda out of her way every time she tried to help her.

"Proud," the doctor said in an undertone.

"Stubborn," Michael said. He noticed her eyes seemed to be going in two different directions at once. "How much painkiller did you give her?" he asked under his breath.

"Enough to knock out a baby rhino," the doctor told him.

"Did you base the dosage on the thickness of her skin?"

"I don't think it's as thick as she wants us to believe."

"I think you're right."

"I'm ready to go," she said regally, swaying before him. He reached out to steady her. "Don't touch me. I can do it myself."

He exchanged a look with the doctor over her head.

The doctor's glance clearly said, *Have fun in hell.*

"I'll take Tyler," Dr. Height said out loud.

Sadie marched out the doors, Michael close behind her.

"Bye, Mike," Wenda called, and then to his irritation added, "Call sometime."

"Call sometime," Sadie said in such an exact imitation of Wenda's syrupy voice that Dr. Height chuckled.

At the first curb she stumbled, and nearly went to her knees. Michael grabbed for her and caught her just in time.

"I said I don't need your help," she said trying to twist away from him.

"Lady—" he took both her shoulders in his hands, and made her look right into his eyes "—let's get something straight right now. You do need my help. Got it?"

She stared at him defiantly for a second, and then her gaze softened and wandered over his shoulder. She nodded, ever so slightly.

"Good," he said, and scooped her light form up in his arms for the rest of the trip to the van.

Behind him he heard Dr. Height's grunt of approval.

He opened the door and put her in, reaching over her to do up her belt. It snapped into place.

"Would you like me to kiss you?"

He was so surprised, he straightened, and banged his head hard on the top of the door.

Boy, would he like it!

But not with Dr. Height looking on, not when it had been brought on by an altered state and not when he was going to have to spend the night under the same roof with her— but not *with* her if he was any kind of a gentleman.

"Well?" she demanded.

Her eyes focussed on his lips with such intensity, his mouth went dry.

"Not right now, Sadie," he said, but it took just about everything he had to say it.

"Humph," she said with surprise. She leaned back and closed her eyes, and began to hum a very raspy little hum.

He strapped the kids in, and said goodbye to their grand-father.

"Good luck," Dr. Height told him, amusement in his voice.

Perhaps because Sadie had started to sing.

"The pony ate my ring, the pony stepped on my hand, and now I'm in a sling, and watching his rear end."

The kids cracked up laughing. Sadie's singing voice was dreadful, raspy and completely out of tune, but Michael couldn't help liking it anyway.

"What is that smell?" Sadie asked.

"Tyler!" the kids and Michael chorused together.

"Well," she said, "am I ever glad it wasn't him who wallowed my ring." And then she started to sing again.

Soon Amber and Tucker were singing the song, too, at

the top of their voices. Even the baby was gurgling along in time.

The song did not develop any more stanzas. But they were able to sing the one they had forty-two times before Michael pulled up in front of the McGee residence.

He leaned over her to help her with her seat belt again.

If she asked him if he was going to kiss her, he'd have to just call up Kate Adams and get her to stay the night.

But this time she didn't ask. As he reached across, her lips, soft as buttercup petals, touched his cheek.

He froze.

But the touch was over almost before it began, so quick that if it was not for the quivering sensation that remained in his stomach, he would not even be sure it had happened.

He glanced sidelong at her.

Her head was back again, her eyes closed, her lips faintly parted.

Inviting him to kiss her back?

That illusion shattered with the gentle snore that trembled off her lips.

Chapter Five

Michael woke up. His back was so sore, it felt like daggers were being run through it.

He looked around, disoriented. The room was beautiful—hardwood floors, hand-woven Finnish rugs, a river-rock fireplace.

And a couch that was not designed for sleeping on, he thought as he rolled off it and stood up slowly.

It was all coming back to him now.

Three kids, a pony and a semi-invalid.

One of those kids had needed a diaper change. The first Michael had ever done. He thought one mandatory diaper change per unmarried bachelor would probably be an effective form of birth control—the whole population of the earth brought to zero in no time.

It could also be used for weight control since one's thoughts did not naturally turn to food after getting through such an ordeal.

But the kids had to eat, and let him know it, whether he had an appetite or not. Tucker eating a hot dog was nearly

as gross as Tyler needing a diaper change. Shreds of bun
that looked like they had been run through the dishwasher
had been all over himself, the table, the chair, the floor *and*
the cloth calendar twelve feet across the kitchen. Mustard,
ketchup and relish in his hair, on his clothes, up his nose,
between his toes *and* on the cat.

And then there was Amber, so solemn and sweet and
grown up. Enough to make a man who'd recently—very
recently—decided never to have children of his own, decide
maybe one or two just like her would be bearable.

Children looked after, the pony had urgently needed a
fence, and he had managed to get that done, with all his
"helpers," just as the light was fading from the sky. He
could have done the job in half the time without the helpers,
but he had not the heart to tell them that. Amber had informed him they always had a bath and bedtime stories.
Tonight, they'd had just had one bedtime story and that had
been the shortest one he could find in their crowded book-
shelf.

He'd tucked them in, remembered the buried treasure in
the pony and gone back out to give the manure a few half-
hearted kicks. Nothing shiny showed up. He was mean
enough to be glad when it didn't.

The semi-invalid was full of painkillers and out like a
light in a too-large man's T-shirt, the only thing she was
able to get on without assistance, which she had refused.
Thank God. Sort of.

He remembered staggering in here, exhausted, planning
to watch TV for a few minutes before finding a bed to sleep
in for the night.

Michael stretched again and then turned and gave the
couch a baleful look. Well, it was his own fault. A six-
foot-one-inch man did not lie down on a five-foot-four-inch

couch without getting a crook in his back. Even a man with a good back to begin with.

He froze when he heard the whimper.

Had that woken him up?

He moved down the dark hall and crashed into a table placed artfully into a small recess. He swore, remembered all the young ears and amended hastily.

"I meant darn."

No one answered. He hoped like hell it wasn't the baby making noises. He wasn't up to that again, just yet. Of course, he wasn't going to feel up to that again for some time, and he didn't think the baby was going to hold off for a week or two just to convenience him.

He peeked in at the baby. Fanny in the air. Thumb in mouth. Eyes closed. Check.

Tuck was in the same room. Upside down in bed. Pajamas half off. Snappy stuck between the bed and wall. Close enough. Check.

Amber's room was the next one down the hall. He peeked in. She was snoring softly. He almost shut the door again when he noticed something clutched tightly in her hand. He tiptoed in.

A lump formed in his throat. Her mom's picture. He pried it gently away, worried about what would happen to the glass if she dropped it or rolled on it during the night. He set it gently on the nightstand beside her, so that the first thing she would see in the morning would be her mother's soft smile.

He was not generally a praying man, but he sent a small plea heavenward before he left her.

Please don't let anything happen to Amber's mom.

Check.

The whimper came again.

That only left Sadie.

He crept down the hall to her room, and tapped lightly on the door. "Sadie?" He looked in.

"Sorry," she mumbled. "Did I wake you?"

"A good thing. A whole night on that couch and by morning you could be trying to peddle me to the circus as the human pretzel. Besides, better you than Tyler. I can't do diaper duty again for a while."

"There's a clothespin on the change table. That helps."

"How?"

"You put it on your nose."

"That's what the clothespin is for? I thought it was part of the diaper fastening system!"

"Nope. Nose. It works for me."

He laughed, imagining her with that clothespin jammed on her cute upturned nose. "I thought, somehow it would be easier for a woman to change a diaper."

"That was a male-chauvinist thing to say."

"Wasn't it? Good thing your slugging hand is out of commission."

"Come closer. My left hook is pretty good, too."

He did move into the shadowy room, to stand right above the bed. She looked small and fragile and incredibly beautiful under a huge and colorful patchwork quilt.

"You have to get closer than that if I'm going to punch you."

He sat on the edge of the bed.

She sighed. "You're not afraid."

"Fearless," he agreed. "I already took out the coffee table, and you're hardly any bigger than that."

"You'll be sorry. I'm tougher than I look."

He already knew that. He watched with amusement as she freed her good hand from under the quilt, formed a fist and thumped him on the upper arm.

He grabbed his arm and bent over. "Sadie," he croaked, "that was my bad arm."

He watched covertly as her eyes got wide. "Bad arm?"

"Ah, the pain," he moaned. "I don't think I can stand it."

"Michael—"

"I may never be able to change another diaper. In fact, I'm pretty sure—"

She caught on that he was pulling her leg, and thumped him again, a lot harder this time.

He straightened up and regarded her with a grin. He'd coaxed a small reluctant smile from her. The pain was less visible in her eyes, but not gone.

"That hand hurts, huh?" he commented.

"Naw."

"Tell the truth."

"What makes you think I'm lying?"

"Your ears twitched."

"They did not!"

"I swear—they did."

"Did they teach you that at policeman school? The ear-twitch method of lie detection?"

"Yes, ma'am, they did. You might as well make a full confession now."

"Okay, so it hurts. A little."

"They're still twitching."

She covered one ear with her good hand and pressed the other into her pillow. "It hurts a bit."

"A bit is only slightly more than a little, and I think if you remove your hands from your ears, we'll see that—"

"Okay, okay. It hurts. Like I held it in an open flame for ten minutes and then asked a school of tap dancers to practice on top of it."

"I'll get you a painkiller."

"No!"

He looked at her. She was so close, he could smell her. It was a nice smell like soap and baby powder. Her eyes were wide, silvered by the moonlight pouring in her window. Her hair was tousled like that of a little farm kid who'd been playing in the hay. The T-shirt was on backward.

"Why not?"

"I don't want to sing for you anymore."

"Come on, Sadie, serenade me."

"What did Dr. Height give me anyway? I behaved very foolishly."

She was blushing. Even in the dark he could see the deep rose moving up her cheeks. Once, it seemed to him, this woman, when she was just a girl, had not worried so much about behaving foolishly. Hadn't she walked just a touch on the wild side?

"I liked it," he said with a grin. "Kind of a catchy tune. Very creative."

"Yeah, well..." she said uncomfortably.

"The painkillers I picked up at the drugstore wouldn't be quite the same potency as the shot the doc gave you. They won't make you do anything you don't want to."

"What makes you think I want to do anything?" she asked sharply.

"Touchy, touchy," he scolded. He took a few extra pillows and stuffed them behind his back, then put his legs up on the bed.

"Ahhh."

"I hope you're comfortable," she said. She'd pulled the covers up around her chin and was eyeing him warily as if she expected to be attacked at any moment.

Or wanted to be. That *they won't make you do anything you don't want to* had elicited a rather strong reaction.

"I have a bad back," he told her. "I fell asleep on the couch, and I'm paying for it now."

"From the accident, Michael? Your back?"

"Yeah. I can't sit for long periods of time anymore. That's why I left the police force. People do not believe how much sitting is involved in police work. You're in a car a lot of the time."

"But not your arm?"

"No. That was a ruse to try and get out of diaper duty."

She made a face at him. "Are you sorry that you're not on the police force anymore? I seem to remember you being very enthusiastic about your career, way back when."

"Oh, I was, way back when. But by the time the accident happened it was just a job. Giving Maybelle Swift a speeding ticket once a week, breaking up kids drinking beer at the Square on Friday night."

"I used to be one of those kids," Sadie said, as if it was something she was vaguely ashamed of.

"Me, too," Michael said, and they both laughed.

"I mouthed off to Hawk Adams once when he caught me having a beer."

"I knew you were a brave girl."

"More like stupid."

"See? Hawk is the kind of guy who was born to be a cop. I don't think I ever mastered that Clint Eastwood squint that says, without one word being spoken, 'Do as I say, or I'm going to kill you. *And* I'm going to enjoy it.'"

She laughed softly, and then looked at him so intently, it took his breath away.

"You're right," she said looking away quickly. "No killer look in those eyes."

"Hawk doesn't really have that old killer look anymore, either. Being married and having two kids has changed him a lot. Interestingly enough, it's made him a better cop. Most of the town was hoping he would run for chief when Bill Nordstrom retired but Hawk said he wasn't cut out for administration.''

"He's one of my favorite people," Sadie said. "Hawk and Kate put me through school. They were kind of the first respectable adults who believed I could make something of myself. Their belief went a long way."

"Sadie, you say that as if you had to rebuild yourself from scratch, and that's not true. You always had something special. Hawk and Kate saw it right away. And I did, too.''

"I was awfully rough around the edges."

"You were real, Sadie. You don't know what a rare and precious thing that is."

"How can you say that? I bleached my hair! I wore too much makeup. I talked like a moll in a bad movie. I'm not even going to mention the clothes."

"Well, I kind of liked that little black leather skirt that you—"

"Oh, be quiet!"

He reached over and laid his hand gently above her breast, over her heart. "I wasn't talking about those kind of things, anyway," he said, aware of the unguarded roughness in his voice. "This is what I was talking about. You shot straight from the heart."

He could feel the beat of her heart beneath his hand, the heated silk of her skin. He snatched his hand away.

"Oh," she said, and then recovered herself quickly. "Tell me about the accident."

A diversionary tactic if he'd ever seen one.

"It takes longer to tell than it took to happen."

"That's okay."

"It was a high-speed chase—my first, by the way. High-speed chases are not exactly typical fare in Sleepy Grove.

Some numskull kid had robbed the drugstore, also not very typical fare for around here. Anyway, Miles Manhurst was chasing him up Main, and I was supposed to set up a road-block at the intersection on Twentieth. But the kid was moving a lot faster than anybody thought, and I had to really step on it to beat him to the intersection. He tried to get through it before me, like somebody trying to outrun the train. He hit my vehicle so hard, it spun around about three times. It exploded on impact.

"The whole thing took about four seconds. I don't re-member anything for a long time after that. About a week. I was burned and hurt my back. I got off lucky, all things considered. Real lucky."

After a long pause, she said, "You're happy now, aren't you?"

At the moment he felt like just about the unhappiest man alive. He was lying in bed beside a gorgeous woman, and if he was any kind of a gentleman, nothing but nothing was going to happen between them tonight.

He tried to push thoughts of kissing her senseless out of his head.

"I like what I'm doing." He hoped she'd ask.

"I saw the article on the house you did. It was beauti-ful."

Even better. She already knew. "Thanks. How did you happen to come across that? I mean *Heritage* isn't exactly the most widely read magazine out there."

This conversation just proved the point a person really could hold two thoughts in their head at once. Because he was still thinking of kissing her, wondering what her lips would taste like underneath his, wondering how to get that T-shirt off over her injured arm—

"Kate sent it to me." She was blushing charmingly. Maybe she was wondering how to get his shirt off with just one arm. "I guess she just thought I'd be interested for some reason. Because of that date she gave me. You know."

"Yeah, I know." He paused. "I liked the second date better. Not the Kate date, but the other one. Where we flew the kite."

"Me, too," she said. "I'd never flown a kite before." She inched a little bit closer to him.

"I remember. You told me." He inched a little bit closer to her.

They weren't touching but he could feel the heat coming from her skin. This was a cruel exercise in discipline.

"You sure have a nice laugh, Sadie McGee," he told her softly. "I hope you use it often."

"Oh, you know," she said awkwardly. "Life."

He felt himself go on red alert. What the hell did that mean? That she didn't laugh often? That she wasn't having fun? Were her and her slick lawyer really talking about stocks instead of chasing each other around the bedroom until one or the other gave up, collapsed from laughter and the sheer delight of being together?

He wondered if he could ask her if they were sleeping together. She'd probably slug him again, but it didn't hurt very much.

"Tell me about your life," he suggested as a warm-up to the question he really wanted to ask.

"It's really quite boring."

Boring? Sadie? Girl he would have voted most likely to bunjee jump from the Space Needle?

"Well, don't tell me any of the boring parts. Skip to the good parts, like what makes you laugh, and what makes your heart beat faster, and what your favorite smell in the whole world is."

"I'm ashamed to say redneck jokes make me laugh. Hard."

"So what? They make me laugh, too."

"Kevin thinks they're coarse and vulgar."

Kevin. Here we go, he thought with grim satisfaction. One step closer to what I really want to know about.

"What does Kevin think is funny?" he asked casually, like a long-lost brother trying to catch up on the news.

"Well..."

She hesitated for long enough that Michael knew she didn't know.

"He likes British humor," she finally spat out desperately.

"Oh. Like Mr. Bean?"

"I guess so."

It was plain to Michael she wouldn't know Mr. Bean if he drove his little yellow Mini right over her.

She was obviously anxious to change the subject. "My favorite smell in the whole world is bread baking. How about you?"

The scent tickling his nostrils right now would be pretty close to the top of his list.

"Wood," he said quickly. "I like the smell of wood when I'm working with it."

He didn't look at her. She didn't look at him. Sitting in that bed as if there was a bolster between them.

"You missed what makes your heart beat faster," he reminded her softly.

"Oh, I don't know. Being scared, I guess."

"Really?" He was sure to load that with lots of meaning. "What about the man whose ring is inside that pony?"

"Kevin?" she said this with such genuine surprise, his question was answered without his having to be desperate enough to ask it.

She wasn't sleeping with him.

"We don't have a romantic relationship. It's more based on mutual respect."

He could have laughed out loud. And she wasn't planning on sleeping with him anytime in the near future, either.

So why was she planning on marrying him?

He wouldn't ask her that. Because he already knew. Sadie thought she had to become a somebody, as if she wasn't more of a somebody than anybody else he'd ever met. She thought marrying this dull lawyer was her ticket to respectability.

But would she be so willing to live with a heart that never beat too rapidly if she experienced it even once? If she lost herself into the throes of passion, would she be willing to throw away her life on Mr. Pom-pom Donkey, then?

"What makes your heart beat faster?" she asked, cautiously.

He smiled, trying not to appear too much like the big bad wolf. *Funny you should ask, my dear.*

"It's beating pretty hard right now."

"Don't, Michael."

So, she knew. She knew if she gave in to this temptation, she might never be able to be happy with the pom-pom. He didn't want to call him Kevin, not even in his own mind.

"You're very beautiful," he told her huskily.

"I am not. Michael don't."

"Doesn't *he* think you're beautiful?"

"Michael—"

"You started it."

"I most certainly did not!"

"You offered to kiss me."

"I was out of my head then!"

"Well, thank you very much."

"Nothing against you."

"Of course not."

"I appreciate your not taking advantage of the condition I was in."

Did that mean she was expecting him to show the same kind of restraint now? he wondered.

It probably still would fall into the taking-advantage category. Officially.

Unofficially, maybe they could have just one little kiss. Just to get her heart beating faster.

"It was more like you taking advantage of me," he told her softly.

She looked narrowly at him.

"You kissed me."

She turned bright red.

"Right here. On my cheek. It felt like an angel brushing its wing against me."

"Oh, really."

"I wonder what a kiss like that would feel like on my lips."

He leaned toward her. She leaned toward him.

"Michael," she whispered.

There was no *don't* on the end this time.

"Sadie," he said back, softly.

That damned horse picked that precise second to nicker loudly. A loud clang, probably a disgruntled kick to the empty metal feed bin, followed.

Sadie reared back from him, slamming her injured hand into his chest on the way. Her face whitened with pain.

If the dog food wagon came by here tomorrow, that pony was doomed, Michael decided.

"Maybe I better have that painkiller after all."

It was on the tip of his tongue to tell her the painkiller

wouldn't work on every kind of pain. It wouldn't work on the kind that was pulling at her heart right now, telling her to taste his lips, telling her laughter was only a kiss away.

"I'll get it for you."

When he came back she was sleeping. Well, he'd taken his time, trying to get one lid on his libido and one off the pills. He'd insisted on a childproof cap.

It was just as well she was asleep. She was sick after all. Hurting. This was no time to press his advantage, if he even had one.

Anyway, who did he think he was, meddling in her life? He thought the lawyer was all wrong for her, but was he prepared to be Mr. Right?

He was just getting on his feet again after the accident. Though he didn't have any money problems, he needed to have purpose. He needed to focus intensively on getting his business going. He had the fire-hall renovation coming up. He remembered the doctor's words this afternoon. *Hopefully,* he had the fire-hall renovation coming up.

He had nothing to offer Sadie. She had no interest in the small and sleepy things of Sleepy Grove, and he had no interest in the glitz and glamour of the city life.

The glitz and glamour of a lawyer's wife.

Somehow he couldn't picture Sadie hosting a charity tea.

But she could picture herself doing it, so who was he to think he knew what she needed more? What would bring her happiness?

He had never really thought of being anyone's Mr. Right before. Even though lots of woman had let him know they wouldn't mind if he ate crackers in their beds—for life.

Wenda, the nurse, was one of them. They'd dated a few times. She'd been interested. He hadn't.

He wasn't sure why. She was bright, good-looking as all get-out, a small-town girl who had no ambition of becoming a big-city lady. She cooked a mean roast-beef dinner, he recalled.

He bet Sadie couldn't boil water without burning it.

But the thing about Wenda, and a lot of the other women he'd dated was that they all seemed to lack something. Originality. It was as if they'd been cut from the same cookie cutter. They dressed the same and wore their hair in imitations of characters on the latest popular TV shows, and *talked* the same. Endless gabble about nothing. Decorating. Trips. Movies. The soaps. Clothes. Not one of them could have made up an impromptu song about a pony's rear end, not even under the influence.

He didn't hold it against them. He just didn't want to be with them. He couldn't always even figure out what they liked about him.

He was tall and moderately good-looking. Was that anything to base a relationship on?

He set the painkiller and the glass of water on the side table. He should go find a bed.

On the other hand, there was a perfectly good one right here. He'd just sit beside her for a few minutes, make sure she didn't need that painkiller, be close if she whimpered anymore in her dreams.

He slid into bed beside her. It was so comfortable. He decided just to close his eyes for a minute.

He sought her good hand under the covers. He was just going to hold it for a second. It curled around his trustingly.

In a minute, he'd get up and find another place to sleep. In a second he'd let go of her hand...

In his dreams the car was on fire and sirens were shrieking around him.

He woke in a sweat.

It was the phone, one of those ones with the shrill squeal for a ring. Thank God it was just the phone.

Everything was wrong. This wasn't his room. He never kept a phone in his room. For this precise reason. He hated to be wakened by the damn things.

It was ringing right in his ear. He scowled, and then found it on the bedside table beside him.

"Yeah?" he said irritably into the receiver.

A long silence that followed woke him more thoroughly than the ringing had. He knew immediately who was calling.

He remembered where he was, too. Someplace he was not supposed to be, no sirree. He slid Sadie a cautious look. She was awake, just barely, and staring at him with horrified fascination. As if she thought maybe he had taken advantage of her while she slept.

Didn't she know that if anything had happened between them, she would know it? And how. He'd know how to get her breathing hard in a way she wouldn't soon forget.

Finally a male voice said, "Mickey?"

"Michael," he corrected, evaluating the voice and disliking it.

"Pardon me. I thought you preferred Mickey."

"Whatever," he said, resisting the temptation to make Sadie have to come up with a nearly impossible explanation. He disliked the man at the other end of the line irrationally.

His voice stank.

Very mature, Michael, he chided himself. Mickey. Whatever.

"Is Sadie there?"

"Right beside me," he said, and gave her a wicked grin before passing her the phone.

She mouthed "Who?"

He waved his arms energetically in the air as if they had pom-poms at the end of them.

Did she actually pale? Poor girl. Why didn't he feel the least bit sorry for her?

"Hello? Oh, hello, Kevin," she said, looking absolute daggers at Michael.

He had a feeling being turned into a pretzel by that couch might well have been the lesser of two evils.

Then again, maybe not. He sighed, not altogether unhappily, and waited for the wrath of Sadie to descend on him.

Chapter Six

"Did you wake me up?" Sadie repeated Kevin's question, a ploy to buy time. "Not really."

Sadie was a woman who prided herself on scrupulous honesty, but she told herself this was not precisely a lie. It was not the ringing of the phone that had woken her, it was Michael's gruff "Yeah?" at such alarmingly close proximity that had made her abruptly shake off sleep.

His voice, sleep roughened like that, had a texture to it that was as alarming as his proximity. *Sexy* was the only word that had entered her sleep-befuddled brain.

"No, I know. I'm not usually a morning person. But you know. Three kids." Another vague statement that wouldn't quite qualify as a lie.

At that moment, Michael shifted on the bed beside her and the springs squeaked outrageously. Had he moved just a hair closer? Wasn't it ridiculous that she suddenly wondered what her own hair looked like?

Pretend this is not happening, she ordered herself tersely. How did you ignore six foot one inches of potently virile male? If she closed her eyes maybe she could pretend this was all a bad dream, at least until she hung up from Kevin.

She closed her eyes. It had the unfortunate effect of making her more aware of Michael's scent.

Which was soapy and clean and spicy and as sexy as his voice growling ''yeah'' first thing in the morning. Baking bread had just moved into second place on her list of lovely smells.

She opened her eyes and glared pointedly at him. He smiled back at her with choirboy innocence, as if he was as shocked and surprised as she was to find himself in her bed.

She waved her hand at him, a universally accepted gesture for *go away*. But if she thought he would have the decency to get out of bed and let her have her conversation in private she was one hundred percent wrong. With deliberate misunderstanding he waved back at her, then stretched out, folded his hands comfortably behind his head and closed his eyes, apparently lost in enjoyment of the early-morning sunlight on his face.

He did look incredibly handsome in the early-morning light. The faintest shadow of whiskers defined his bone structure, making him look dangerously rugged and appealing, like an old-time pirate.

She twisted, turning her back to him. *There* she thought, as if she was a dieter who had just won a battle over a chocolate éclair.

''What?'' she asked Kevin. ''I missed that. My brother home? Of course not. Who? Oh, that's not my brother. It's just the neighbor.'' She tried to imbue the word *neighbor* with all sorts of meaning—a doddering little old man arriving with his rake in one hand and a casserole in the other. It was a tall order to put that much into one word, and Meryl Streep she wasn't. She could tell by Kevin's tone she'd failed to defuse the threat. He knew that voice didn't belong to an old man with a rake and a casserole.

"He told you he was Mickey? I'm sure you misunderstood. He's here so early because I had a small accident. He's just helping me out. For a little while. Until I make different arrangements."

She snuck a quick peek over her shoulder. Michael opened his eyes and raised his eyebrows at her, meaning *good luck.*

She was annoyed at herself for looking. Well, she told herself, even a dieter could *look* at the éclair.

She made her voice turn to ice after Kevin's next question. "I'm going to pretend you didn't ask me if he was in bed with me," she said so coolly that her voice could have turned Kool-Aid to Popsicles.

Somehow, Michael's thumbs-up gesture was in her range of vision. Were her eyes sneaking back that way without her permission?

"Oh. You were just kidding."

"Very British humor," Michael murmured, and sounded exactly like Prince Charles.

Her good hand was unfortunately occupied holding the phone, her palm clamped down hard over the mouthpiece, or she would have hit him. On his bad arm. And it wouldn't have been playful this time.

"I broke my hand…a pony stepped on it. *P-o-n-y.* Is the connection bad at your end? Yes, it hurts…yes, it's very disabling…yes, it's going to cause a problem in getting the proposal done, not to mention child care… You'll what?… *No.*"

Kevin was offering to take a few days off and come down and help her out. She didn't want him to come here.

Though she had sworn she would not look at him again until she put this phone down, she glanced at the man beside her. Because of him? All the more reason for Kevin to come, and come quickly.

But what if Kevin wanted to meet her parents? What if he asked about the ring? What if he didn't like the kids? What if they didn't like him? What if Amber called him Pom-pom Donkey to his face? Or Michael? She could probably trust Amber.

Amber came in, rubbing her eyes, but she came fully awake when she saw them in bed together.

"I'll call you back," Sadie said and hung up without waiting for Kevin to say goodbye, and in the nick of time, too.

Because Amber asked loudly, "Michael, what are you doing in Auntie Angel's bed?"

"She was having bad dreams last night," Michael said, smooth as the brand of peanut butter Amber insisted on. "I didn't want to leave her alone."

"That's a good idea," the little traitor said approvingly.

Michael smiled angelically at Sadie.

"Does your hand hurt, Auntie Angel?"

"Just a little."

"Is she lying?" Amber asked, turning to Michael.

He nodded. "She's trying to be brave."

"My mom says you don't have to be brave," Amber informed them. "You can cry if you want to."

Oh, how I love Samantha, Sadie thought. I wish I could cry when I wanted to. Like right now.

"Your mom's a very wise lady," Michael said.

"I know," Amber replied. "I'll make you breakfast if you like. I make it for Mommy and Daddy sometimes and they eat it in bed."

"No," Sadie said too quickly, and saw the flash of hurt in Amber's eyes. But she remembered all too well Amber's last attempt at cooking. Of course, the fire department was a lot closer this time. Which brought her to the second point: she wanted Michael out of this bed, not settling in for breakfast.

Now that she was allowing herself to look at him, she leveled a glance at him that would have stripped paint. Just to let him know he was not off the hook. He ignored her.

"What do you make Mommy and Daddy for breakfast?" he asked Amber.

"Waffles in the toaster. With the real maple syrup that's only for special."

"Well, today feels pretty special to me," Michael said. "How does it feel to you, Sadie?"

Oh, he was too clever! If she said it didn't feel special now, she'd hurt Amber's feelings.

"Very special," she said. "Waffles sound wonderful, Amber."

Amber trotted off happily.

"You forgot to ask her to bring you the paper," she told him sarcastically.

"Amber," he called, "could you see if—"

"Stop it! What are you doing?"

"I was going to ask Amber to bring us the paper."

Us. As though they were going to sit in bed like some old married couple looking through the paper. Sports for him. Home Styles for her.

"That's not what I meant, and you know it. What are you doing here?"

"Waiting for my waffle?" he said hopefully.

Don't let him make you laugh, she warned herself. "Let me be more precise. What are you doing in this bed? Why did I wake up in this bed with you beside me?"

"I fell asleep here. I didn't mean to, but I didn't feel I could leave you, whimpering like a little lost puppy, so I just climbed in with you. Purely altruistic."

"I did not whimper like a little lost puppy!"

"How do you know?"

That was a good question. How did she know? "And even if I did, it was completely inappropriate for you—"

"Completely inappropriate? Sadie, you sound like an old schoolmarm. I remember you with a bolder side, walking a little closer to the edge—"

"Don't try and sidetrack me. Because—"

"Because you're going to give me hell, no matter what. Okay." He folded his arms across the hard expanse of a wide chest and mischief danced in eyes that were impossibly, seductively, criminally attractive. "Okay. Let me have it. Poor guy comes over here and watches your kids, changes diapers, cleans hot dogs off the walls, sifts through pony poop, and what do I get? Blasted. Okay, go ahead. I'm ready."

He was making her laugh. Not out loud yet, but a kind of a trembling in her stomach.

"The point is you shouldn't have been in bed with me." Her voice sounded stern. Her face was set in stern lines. Her stomach quivered like that proverbial bowl of jelly of Santa Claus fame.

"Okay. You're right, I shouldn't have been. I should have done the decent thing and ignored the cries and moans of a fellow human being in pain."

"You can't sleep in the same bed with someone that you hardly know!" There. Just the right tone of righteous indignation.

"I thought we were getting to know each other fairly well. I have a fair repertoire of redneck jokes. Also, I do bake bread."

"I am in no mood for jokes, and you do not bake bread. Your ears twitched *and* your nose grew." He was getting to her. Without wanting to, she was being drawn into his light banter.

"Okay. Not yet. But I have, on occasion, considered learning."

"What occasion was that?" she asked suspiciously.

"I don't remember exactly. But sometime recently, I did tell myself, 'Michael, you should take up making bread.'"

"Was that very recently? Like last night?" He was just kidding her. There was no point entertaining the absurdly romantic notion that he would really try baking a loaf of bread just because it happened to be her favorite smell. Her ex-favorite smell.

"It might have been last night."

"Michael, you are missing the point," she said, but most of her exasperation was dissipated. This man's charm was downright frightening.

And she was sure he had enough women hovering around him to prove it, if Wenda was any example, and Sadie would bet she was.

"No, I'm not missing the point. You think it was inappropriate that you and I shared a bed, but it was an emergency—"

"Not quite like being stuck together in a blizzard with just one blanket," she told him.

"Well, no, maybe not, though I wouldn't mind trying that sometime, if you're up to it. It was more like my back hurt, and I was tired, and you were restless and in pain, and it seemed like the convenient thing to do. And practical."

Convenient and practical. What had she wanted from him? The admission that he couldn't tear himself away from her?

"Anyway, absolutely nothing happened. I didn't lift up your T-shirt and have a peek or anything. You did kind of get tangled up in the blanket once, and the T-shirt rode up a little high, but I covered you up in no time. Nice legs, by the way.''

"You're incorrigible," she squeaked.

"Now I would have considered it inappropriate if I kissed you and you didn't want me to. But I think if I kissed you, you'd want me to."

This was going in all kinds of directions she did not want it to go. "My boyfriend called this morning!" she reminded him.

"Ah, the real problem."

She eyed him suspiciously. "Kevin is not the problem here."

"Am I mistaken or has Kevin been demoted? Wasn't he almost officially your fiancé just yesterday?"

"You are severely trying my patience."

"You never had any patience, Sadie. Remember when your kite string got all knotted up? Out comes a jackknife, right out of your pocket—"

"Michael!"

"Okay. You win. I am the problem. I slept in the wrong bed. Punish me. Lock me in a room with Tyler and a dirty diaper, or Tucker and a hot dog. Make me spend a night in the same bed with you and forbid me even one little kiss."

"Don't say things like that." She could feel the heat moving up her cheeks.

"It's only the truth. You have very luscious lips. They practically beg a man to kiss them."

He was teasing her. She could tell by the light in his eyes. He was trying to drive her over the edge. What he had succeeded in doing was making her look at his own lips.

Would she have slept a wink if she knew he was in bed

beside her, a breath away? Would the thought of his lips have tortured her all night long?

Oh, this was going in directions she could not allow it to go. She was not a woman free to be thinking of other men's lips.

"I really do appreciate your help," she said gracefully, "I'm not saying I don't."

"What are you saying, Sadie?"

"It was just a shock to wake up with you here. And the phone ringing. And Kevin there."

"A shock is good for you. Gets the blood flowing. Makes life seem like it holds some adventure, not just the same old thing day in and day out."

"Now I'm supposed to thank you, I suppose?" she said, and she could not keep the wry grin off her lips.

"Well, if you insist—"

She picked up the pillow, one-handed, and hit him with it. He wrestled it away from her and thumped her over the head. One-armed, she was at a disadvantage but she still found another pillow and fought him back. Fought him until she was breathless with laughter, and her good arm ached. One more last swipe. She hit him square across the cheek. The air turned white with feathers.

"Look what you've done now," she said, lying back breathlessly and watching the feathers drift down.

"You did it."

"I know. But you made me."

He was right beside her, his shoulder touching hers.

"Yeah," he said, "look what I've done now." And he turned and looked at her.

For a stunned moment, looking at him, she felt like she knew something deep within her. A secret about the universe. A secret about herself and about him. For a moment, she wanted this to last forever, them lying on the bed, the feathers floating down, their eyes locked together.

"Oh, Michael," she whispered. She wanted to tell him how she had missed him. She wanted to tell him how, when he'd been hurt, thoughts of him had filled her every waking moment. She wanted to tell him that the years in between seemed like a desert now. How all she'd accomplished suddenly seemed like nothing.

She gave herself a quick shake. It was ridiculous. Just a moment of magic trying to steal her sanity away from her.

"Waffles," Amber said. She stood in the doorway with a leaning tower of waffles and looked at the feathers. "I hope you had fun," she said sternly, "'cause my mommy is going to be mad."

The baby started crying. Tucker wandered in with Snappy in a headlock.

With a promise to be right back, Michael got up and went for the baby. From the other room she could hear him scolding Tyler about the condition of his diaper. A few minutes later he was back, the baby riding happily in the crook of his arm.

Tucker and Amber were in bed wistfully eyeing the waffles.

"Let's share," Michael suggested, plunking the baby down on the bed. "Come on, everybody on the bed."

Two plates. Six waffles, five people, two forks and a bed full of kids and feathers.

Every time one of them moved, a cloud of white went up and they had to pick the feathers out of the syrup. The kids laughed until they cried.

And they adored Michael. She watched and felt the heaviness ache inside her. Of wanting.

She knew what she had to do.

Call Kevin back and tell him to get down here. And help her.

Michael O'Bryan's easy charm had broken her heart once before. He hadn't meant to, she was sure. He'd just been being himself, just like he was now.

He hadn't known how it made her yearn for things she had never had. He couldn't know how deep inside she didn't think she'd ever have the things other people seemed to have.

Love. Laughter. Some semblance of normalcy.

After Michael, the first time, she'd started wishing for something else.

Just to get by with her heart intact.

Just to live with an absence of pain.

Good grief, had she chosen Kevin not because of what she felt for him, but the exact lack of feeling she felt?

For her, somehow, strong feelings were equated with turmoil. And she'd had enough of that to last her a lifetime.

Now she wanted something else. Peace. Order. Security. Maybe even respect. Okay. Definitely respect.

And she had all those things in her life in Seattle. Since her involvement with Kevin she'd even been invited to lunch with people who would have never noticed her before.

It had seemed like heady stuff at the time. Lunch at ZeClub with Marilyn Van De Wharton. Shopping in exclusive boutiques with Kevin's sister, Priscilla. Being asked to be the promotions director of this year's charity drive for the hospital by Mrs. Thomas Makalardy herself.

It had seemed heady at the time. Yes indeed.

Why did it pale in comparison to this?

Here she was in the very middle of absolute chaos. Her hand encased in white plaster, pancake syrup dribbling onto a priceless quilt, feathers floating all around her like indoor snow, a pony outside bleating his hunger.

And the most gorgeous man in the world balancing a baby on one knee, a small boy on the other, a bite of waffle in one hand, a little girl's heart in the other.

"Oh, dear," she said. "I am in big, big trouble."

"Pardon?" he asked her, looking up from beneath a shock of thick hair that she had an urge to push back off his forehead.

"I said I hope I find my ring in the pony's rubble."

"You did not, Auntie Angel."

Why was it every time she told a lie, even a teeny tiny one, she got caught?

"You don't have the face for it," he said, as if she'd asked out loud. "Don't ever play poker."

"You said you were in big trouble, Auntie Angel. How come?"

"Oh, I just have so much work to do, and I need both hands to do it with."

His eyes were laughing at her. *Liar, liar,* they said.

"We'll help," Amber said. "Won't we, Uncle Michael?"

Great. *Uncle* Michael. And Auntie Angel. Terrific.

"Actually, *Uncle* Kevin will be coming to help."

"Who?" Amber asked.

Michael leaned over and whispered to her.

She scrunched up her face. "Oh, him."

"You've never even met him," Sadie said defensively.

"I know, but my daddy said—"

"All right. I've already heard what your daddy had to say."

Amber brightened. "Could I tell that man what happened to his ugly ring that he gave you? Please?"

The traitor coming out in her niece again. Resisting calling Kevin Uncle, showing ghoulish delight in telling him the fate of a ring that had been in his family circa Plymouth Rock.

"I think I may need one of those painkillers," Sadie said weakly.

"Tut, tut," Michael said "Addiction setting in."

"What's 'diction?" Amber asked. A new word to add to her already-astonishing vocabulary.

It's what that man's eyes could make me feel in just about no time flat, Sadie answered her niece silently.

Something to be fought at all costs, the giving up of control to forces outside of yourself.

She'd come too far and worked too hard to throw it all away on a pair of dark eyes fringed by impossibly thick lashes. A mouth that smiled so easily, revealing straight white teeth.

He was not asking her to throw anything away, she reminded herself sharply.

It didn't matter if he did ask.

She was strong and independent. She had vowed she would never be the kind of woman who threw it all away for a man.

Not even if it might be delightful fun.

She remembered, too late, about McGees and their cursed bad luck when it came to making vows.

An educated sophisticated woman reduced to superstition.

That was why she should have never come back here.

That was why she had to bring part of her world here—quick.

She looked up, once more, into the amused eyes that rested on her face.

She had a sinking feeling *her* world was nearly lost already.

"Okay, troops," he said. "Auntie Angel looks worn-out. Amber, plates. Tucker, utensils. Tyler, toilet. Oh, I see you have it. Strapped right on. Good man. Forward march. Next stop, the pony pen for poop patrol."

He turned at the door and gave her the sexiest wink she had ever seen.

Chapter Seven

"Here's the paper, Auntie Angel."

"Thanks, honey." Sadie put the baby in his playpen, then took Sleepy Grove's biweekly newspaper from Amber. She opened the dining room window to let some of the burned toast odor out, and then with a little sigh, sank down at the dining room table. Three days had passed since her accident. She was amazed by all the things she could now manage with one hand, and amazed by how time-consuming it could be to do the simplest task.

"Scoot, Tucker," she said when she felt a little metal car drive over her ankle. "Go get dressed." She supposed she should supervise his outfit selection, but she loved the combinations he picked for himself—wild, loud colors, mismatched socks and crazy hats, from baseball caps to Mickey Mouse ears.

"Is our ad in there?" Amber asked eagerly.

Sadie shot her niece a suspicious look. "I was just going to look."

She went directly to Lost and Found. Michael had promised to put an ad in about the pony.

Apparently it had been on the local radio stations, too, but she had not heard it, nor had she had any calls.

"Found," she read, "mean pony—small eyes, eats lots, bites children. To claim, call Michael. Board and damages owed."

"Is the ad in there?" Amber asked again.

"Yes, it is," she said, biting her lip to keep from laughing. She should be steaming mad.

"I helped write it," Amber said proudly.

"Somehow I could tell." Which part had her niece contributed. Found?

"Has that pony ever bitten one of you?" Sadie demanded, trying to work up some proper temper.

"Well, he did kind of nibble on Tyler's hair one day. I think he thought it was hay." Amber giggled.

The giggle stopped Sadie's efforts at anger cold. Something wonderful was happening to her niece. The little girl was coming out to play. Amber actually laughed. And often. Still...

"This is a terrible ad, Amber," she said sternly. "It has lies in it."

"Well, if we said he was a wonderful, gentle pony, lots of people might claim him, even if he really wasn't theirs. Everybody would want him."

At that moment the shaggy head belonging to the pygmy equine in question popped right through the open dining room window.

Sadie shrieked in surprise, dropped the paper and leapt up. The pony regarded her thoughtfully, then took a large bite out of the African violet that sat on the windowsill.

Sadie picked up the paper and swatted him. The pony seemed to think being swatted with a paper added distinctly to the culinary pleasure of African violet, because he closed his eyes and chewed complacently.

"Shoo," Sadie shouted. She thwacked him again. He tilted his head to one side.

"He wants you to do that side, too." Amber hooted with delight.

Sadie obliged him. "Get!"

Amber dissolved into laughter, rolling on the floor and holding her stomach.

"Oh, sorry." Michael's head appeared beside the pony's in the open window. He deftly dodged the rolled-up paper. "Hey!"

Ah, yes, where there was trouble, Michael was soon to follow.

It was the first time Sadie had seen him today. The sight of him, in his flannel shirt, his hair still wet from the shower, made something glow warm as red coals inside of her.

She was wearing her nicest jeans, even though it had been absolute hell to get the snap done up, and a designer tank top with a silk shirt thrown *carelessly* over it. She slid the paper onto the table and tucked a stray hair behind her ear.

Michael peered cautiously back in the window. "Don't hit me."

"You might like it!" Amber squealed. "Pom-Pom did."

"I might like it," Michael said, arching his eyebrows wickedly at Sadie.

Sadie folded her arms over her chest, as if that would ward off his charm. She absolutely hated it when his eyes danced with laughter like that.

"Why is that pony out of his pen?" she asked, forcing the stern note.

"He slipped out the gate while I was digging for diamonds," Michael said. "I think he's figured out the latch."

He hadn't stayed overnight a second time, at Sadie's insistence. But he came over first thing in the morning to help with the kids, phoned at least once during the day to make sure everything was okay and reappeared around bedtime to help with baths.

She was, to her own uneasy dismay, coming to count on him. Looking forward to his unannounced appearances, even to the sound of his voice over the phone. She felt something like Amber must, almost giddy with it. Dressing up for him. Fiddling with her hair.

Not that he seemed to notice. She might as well have stayed with those so-easy-to-put-on sweatpants.

"Nice top," he said with an easy grin that made her wonder if he knew she was waiting for him to notice, knew she had dressed for him.

"Oh, this old thing," she said, which was an absolute lie, the kind she abhorred in women.

Then she just said "thank you," but even that came out all wrong, as if she were some silly schoolgirl who had just been noticed by her pop idol.

"I bet you had a devil of a time getting into those jeans."

"It wasn't that hard," she said haughtily.

"Anytime you need any help..." He grinned evilly, lifted that expressive eyebrow again and twirled an imaginary mustache.

Thank God Kevin was arriving tomorrow.

"Did you find the ring?" she asked anxiously.

"Do you mean this ring?" In a gloved hand he held out the ring.

It winked at her brightly. She had been waiting for this moment for days. Why didn't she feel overjoyed?

"Oh." She reached for it, and then changed her mind.

It was shiny as could be in the places where gunk wasn't stuck to it.

Michael laughed when she recoiled from the ring. "I'll bring it around. Amber, come give me a hand with Pom-Pom."

When he came in the back door he was by himself. Amber, visible through the window, was lying on the pony's back, her arms around his solid neck.

It was like a breath of fresh air entered the room with Michael. Energy. Vitality. The room came suddenly to life.

"How did you manage this morning?" he asked.

"Fine. The toaster only takes one hand. Amber holds the toast still while I butter it."

He sniffed the air.

"Believe me, I can burn toast with two good hands, too. Look, Michael, we need to talk about that ad."

Tucker streaked by them, an amazing blaze of color, a long neon ski cap on his head.

"That kid has flair, doesn't he?" Michael asked admiringly.

"The ad," she said, tapping her toe.

"Haven't had a single call."

"And no wonder! 'Mean. Bites children. Damages owed.'"

"He did step on your hand."

"But not maliciously."

"Oh, a pony mind reader. You could make a lot of money doing that. I saw a program once where—"

"I already make a lot of money! And I don't have to be around long-haired pigs to do it." She felt instantly remorseful for calling Pom-Pom a long-haired pig. He was such a gentle little soul. She was sure he really had not meant to stand on her hand.

"You're gorgeous *and* you make a lot of money?" Michael asked with grave interest. "You must be fighting them off with a stick."

"Fighting who off with a stick?"

"Why, eligible bachelors, of course."

"I am not exactly eligible myself." Still, she could feel a blush heating her cheeks. Michael thought she was good-looking. It was something he let her know often, and it was silly to still be pleased every single time. But she was. Inordinately.

"You," she said accusingly, before he managed to completely distract her, "are trying to avoid the topic of the ad. Nobody is going to answer an ad like that."

He came closer, reached out and patted a rooster tail she had tried desperately and unsuccessfully to tame this morning. "There," he said.

She loved his scent. Clean and utterly manly. She'd like to touch his hair, too, but he didn't have a convenient rooster tail sticking up.

Oh! She was completely distracted again.

"The pony," she croaked.

"If you had a pony, and you loved him, and he was lost, wouldn't you answer any ad that said a pony had been found? Wouldn't you know Pom-Pom's heart, even if the ad said he was mean? Wouldn't you want him back, even if you did have to pay board and damages? Wouldn't you be willing to be responsible for him? If that ad stops the real owner from claiming their pony then they don't deserve him."

"And you do?"

"Not me. Sometimes, owning things isn't about having the piece of paper that says you own it. It's about how you feel in your heart toward it. Sometimes, things just belong to you."

He held her gaze for a long time, and she wondered, panic-stricken, just how close he was to owning her heart.

He chose that moment to fish her ring out of his pocket. He held it out to her.

She stared at it. Did this ring belong to her? She spun away from the question in his eyes and filled a pot with water. "Drop it in there."

He did.

"How long do you suppose I need to cook it for?" she muttered, watching the ring sink to the bottom of the pot.

"I don't know. The pony seemed to think it was okay raw."

She didn't say it out loud but she thought, Oh, Michael, I always want to laugh when I'm with you. Just like Amber, I'd almost forgotten how.

"I meant to sterilize it," she said, rolling her eyes.

"I don't know. How long do you sterilize jam jars for?"

"Jam jars?" There it was. That reminder again. How far apart their worlds were. He still thought women made jam.

"I don't make jam," she told him stiffly.

"Don't you? It seems to me if I'm willing to learn to make bread, you have to be willing to learn to make jam."

And there, just like that, he'd erased it again. Made the difference small and something to laugh at.

"You go first," she invited. "When I see the bread, I'll provide the jam."

"Homemade."

"I don't think I have too much to worry about."

"That's where you are wrong. I bought a bread book yesterday. *The Bachelor's Bread Making Bible.*"

"You are an awful liar."

"I swear it's true—$22.95 at Casey's Wordworks, downtown Sleepy Grove."

She eyed him warily. It couldn't possibly be true. What

an absurd title for a book. What a ridiculous amount to pay for it. He was making it all up. It didn't matter if it was true anyway. Kevin was coming. Sam and Mickey were due home soon.

"I have some things to do today," he said. "Do you need anything? Groceries?"

"No, you've stocked us up enough to last for a while. And people keep bringing casseroles by. It's wonderful. I'm not going to have to cook a single meal."

"See? Sometimes small towns aren't so bad."

Sadie sighed. Every single neighbor who had dropped by with a casserole had seemed so genuinely pleased to see her, so interested in her life in Seattle. One of her old classmates had dropped by, a girl she had remembered as particularly snooty. But Fiona had been as nice as could be, a plump baby on one hip, her casserole in her other hand. They'd actually had coffee together and found things to talk about.

Not one person had made her feel like she came from the wrong side of the tracks.

Was it possible they had never made her feel that way? That she had made herself feel it?

"What's wrong, Sadie?"

He was standing very close to her. He lifted her chin gently in his hand.

"I just feel a little mixed-up sometimes."

He dropped his head.

Really, she had plenty of time to get out of his way. His eyes had telegraphed her exactly what was coming next.

But she didn't get out of his way. She closed her eyes and felt the first brush of his lips on hers.

And it felt wonderful. Exhilarating. Exactly the way homecoming is supposed to feel.

She allowed him to part her lips. She felt as though she

was dry tinder, he the spark. Ignition. She was going up in flames, being consumed by his fire. And it was wonderful. Headier than wine. More thrilling than white-water rafting.

Nature commanded her to return his kiss, to wrap her arms wantonly around the strength of his neck, to pull him closer to her, where she could feel the beating of his heart within the wall of his hard chest.

Madness.

With every scrap of will she possessed she forced herself to open her eyes and pull away from him. She was panting lightly. Her heart was bounding like a rabbit over open ground with the hounds in hot pursuit.

He took a step toward her. She stepped warily back. If they started again, it wasn't going to be that easy to stop next time.

"That didn't help," she told him.

"My morning feels helped quite a lot." His tone was easy, but his eyes were hot and hungry.

"It didn't help how mixed-up I feel!"

"Oh, that. I don't intend to help you with that." He put his hand to his hair and raked it back off his forehead, far more tensely than he was willing to show her.

He grinned at her, then turned away and was out the back door. It swished softly shut behind him. She went and stood at the window, watching him cross the yard, studying him as he paused to throw a ball to a colorfully costumed Tucker before he stopped and dropped on his knee to speak to Amber for a moment.

She could yell at him to never come back. But he might listen. Like last time.

And for a moment, watching him in the yard with the kids, everything she had ever wanted in the whole world seemed to be hers. A breathtakingly handsome man, children laughing and playing in the autumn sunshine, a pony munching away behind a little picket fence.

All illusion, she told herself crossly. The kids weren't hers. The pony wasn't hers. And he most certainly was not hers.

Even if she did feel that strange sense of ownership way down deep in her heart.

The water started to boil on the stove and she turned away from him and went and looked into the roiling water.

He'd gone and wrecked everything now.

Because this ring would never feel like hers. She had to give it back.

Did that mean it was okay to kiss him again? She sighed at her own stupidity. There was no point jumping from one man to another like a flea off a camel. Michael had shown her her relationship with Kevin was not workable, but that didn't mean she had to have a relationship with *him*.

Why not? her little inner voice needled her.

"Because," she answered it out loud, "he—"

Kisses like a house on fire.

"Lies!" she told herself sanctimoniously. Look at that ad for the pony. Look at the lie about the bread book. How would you ever know when a man like that was kidding and when he wasn't?

It would be absolutely exasperating.

With great purpose she took the phone book out of the kitchen drawer and looked up the number.

"Casey's Wordworks," a cheerful voice answered.

"I'm looking for a book called *The Bachelor's Bread Making Bible.*" She waited for the snort of disbelieving laughter.

"Sold my last one yesterday. I'm having trouble keeping that one in stock."

In Sleepy Grove? Men in Sleepy Grove were baking bread?

"Do you want me to hold one for you when my order comes in?"

"No, no thank you," she said weakly. She ordered herself to hang up. *Hang up, Sadie.*

"Was there something else, ma'am?"

It was stupid. Kevin was coming. She was leaving. It was stupid.

"Do you have anything…" She hesitated, then blurted it out. "Do you have anything on making jam?"

Kate Adams came over in the afternoon with her children, Becky and Ethan. Ethan, six, was the spitting image of his father with his solid build, thick dark hair and his flashing silver eyes. Becky had her mother's coloring—freckles and auburn hair—but an impish face all her own.

The pony was a huge hit.

"Hawk read me Michael's ad in the paper this morning," Kate told her. "We nearly died laughing. Any takers?"

"Oh, sure."

Fall was in the air, and they both had on sweaters as they sat on the veranda and sipped coffee and watched the children. Amber now considered herself an accomplished horse person. She could coax the pony into a slow walk around the yard with enough frantic beating of her feet against his sides. Ethan was so jealous, his eyes were spitting fire.

"Those two never get along," Kate said with a sigh.

"Then they're probably going to grow up and get married," Sadie said.

"It's funny you should say that. Hawk says the very same thing. What's the word on Sam?"

"They're testing relatives for a match."

"You know we're all praying for her," Kate said, reaching out and giving Sadie's hand a squeeze. "It's been so hard on the kids. It's been a long time since I've seen Amber so much herself. The last time we were over, she didn't even fight with Ethan—just ignored him, which nearly made him crazy. She seems happy today."

"Michael makes her forget her problems for a little while." She nodded at the pony. "A case in point. He's good for her."

"And so are you," Kate said with a smile.

"Me?"

"You're helping her believe in love again."

That was funny, Sadie thought, since she had long since relegated love in her own life to the discarded fairy-tale bin.

"Kate, could I ask you a favor? I mean I probably shouldn't, but do you think—" She fished the ring out of her pocket and held it out to Kate.

Kate had an astounding gift. She was often able to "see things" by holding an object that belonged to another person. This talent had entwined her and Sadie's lives several years ago.

"It's not Sam's, is it?" Kate asked.

"No. You told me once it doesn't work like that."

"Sometimes I wish it did. How I'd like to tell that little girl over there there's going to be a happy ending."

Kate sighed, then took the ring and looked at it. "It's lovely, Sadie. How on earth did you get it to sparkle like this?"

"A little digestive juice of pony," Sadie told her, and then filled her in on exactly how her hand had come to be broken. About how the ring came to be in her possession, she said nothing. Kate didn't ask, and the silence stretched out between them.

"Do you feel anything from it?" Sadie asked anxiously.

Kate looked at Sadie carefully, glanced at the children and then sat back and closed her eyes, dropping the ring lightly from one hand to another. After a while, she took the ring and squeezed it lightly in her hand.

She opened her eyes. Shrugged.

"Sadie, I don't get anything from it. It's the oddest thing. I mean obviously the ring is very old and has some history, but I get absolutely nothing. It's like nobody owns it."

Oh! How Sadie wished she hadn't chosen that particular phrase.

"Kevin gave it to me."

"Your lawyer friend?"

Sadie nodded. "He's asked me to marry him."

Kate watched her closely, without comment.

"I thought I was going to. I mean, me, Sadie McGee, a lawyer's wife. Can you imagine? I get invited to all these high-society things—"

Her voice faltered when she heard how she sounded, like an overawed little girl invited for tea with the queen.

That was probably how Diana had felt when Charles first looked her way—and look what had happened to them!

"Do you love him?"

Trust Kate to cut right to the heart of the matter.

"What's that got to do with it?" Sadie sang lightly.

Kate did not smile.

"I just feel all mixed-up," Sadie admitted for the second time that day. She fiddled with her sling. Her eyes rested on where Michael had signed her cast, and then to the delight of the children, drawn a cartoon of a wild-eyed pony. She sighed. "I feel like I should have never come back here."

"You had to come back here. You can't move forward until you've moved on."

"Kate, I don't want to be a little nobody from Sleepy Grove, Idaho, all my life."

"You were never a little nobody," Kate told her with such genuine feeling that it brought tears smarting behind Sadie's eyes. "But you see, if you don't know that in your heart, then it doesn't matter where you go, or what job you do, or even who you marry. Don't you know it yet, Sadie? It's all for nothing if you don't know inside you your own value. The education, the job, the lawyer loving you—"

"Oh, I don't know if he loves me."

"That's usually why a man asks a woman to marry him. Don't you believe you're lovable, Sadie? I've always thought it was one of your most recognizable qualities."

"You did?"

"If this man has asked you to marry him, it's because he loves you. And if you don't love him back, what a terrible disservice you would be doing him, and yourself."

Trust Kate to articulate almost exactly the doubts that had been surfacing in her own mind.

"I don't think he loves me, *exactly*," Sadie said. "We kind of have our work in common."

And what else, she asked herself?

"And we like to do the same things."

"Such as?"

"We go out for fancy dinners, go to live theater, rent movies." Her mind chose that moment to shove the memory of her and Michael eating waffles in her bed into her mind.

And it was followed quickly by another memory from the file—her and Michael collapsing in a heap after they'd flown that kite together.

"Kate," she said tiredly, "I haven't felt so mixed-up since…well, since a long time ago."

Since Michael had been injured and she had kept vigil

at his bedside, and tortured herself about all the time they had lost and wondered if she had made the right decision way back when.

But what was the use of thinking about it? She'd been far too young back then to be thinking seriously about a mate for life.

But she didn't have that excuse now.

Isn't that why she'd agreed to think about Kevin's offer? Didn't she know the time was right? To begin to think of things other than ad campaigns and proposals, and the never-ending office politics?

Her gaze fell on the two babies playing happily in the sand pile just to the right of the veranda stairs.

Weren't there other things as important, and as fulfilling? In her heart didn't she know it?

Why had she never asked Kevin how he felt about babies and children? Because she had known it would be wrong? In her heart of hearts she had always known she would never be having babies with him.

Everything he offered appealed to her. Because it was safe and orderly and sensible.

And none of those things had anything to do with love.

"She's eating something," Sadie noticed suddenly and leapt up and ran down the stairs. She fished a chain and medallion out of Becky's mouth. Becky thanked her by chomping down hard on the fingers of her good hand.

She studied the chain. It was beautiful. Simple. Gold. A St. Christopher's medal on the end of it.

"Is this yours?" she asked Kate, going slowly up the steps and handing it to her.

Kate started with surprise when the chain touched her hand. She stared at it and then slowly dropped it from hand to hand.

"It's not, though Hawk has one very similar to it."

After a long look at Sadie, she closed her eyes. When she opened them again, there were tears shining behind them.

"What?" Sadie demanded. "What did you see?"

Kate said nothing, but she stood up and fastened the chain gently around Sadie's neck. "This," she said softly, "belongs to you."

Amber came running up. "Ethan won't give me my turn on Pom-Pom," she yelled. "He—"

She stopped and looked at the chain Sadie was fingering dazedly.

"Where'd you get that, Auntie Angel? Uncle Michael lost it yesterday. We looked everywhere for it."

Kate met Sadie's astonished look and smiled softly.

"Tell Ethan to get off my pony!" Amber insisted. "He's had a long enough turn. I hate him!"

Kate rolled her eyes, and hummed the wedding march under her breath as she left the porch to go deal with her son.

Chapter Eight

Kevin's car pulled up in front of Mickey and Sam's house the following day. Sadie, Amber and Tucker were reading a story on the front porch, cuddled together among the soft colorful cushions of the white wicker furniture.

Sadie stood up. She smiled when she noticed two teenage boys going by on their bicycles had stopped to gawk.

"That's an ugly car, Auntie Angel," Amber said of the Mercedes. "It's a yucky color."

"Uggie, yuggie." Tucker practiced his vocabulary from his post behind Sadie's leg.

The car was gray, subdued and elegant. Not generally a color anyone would take such exception to. Sadie shot her niece a look. Amber's features were set in decidedly belligerent lines.

"Remember what we talked about," Sadie warned in a whisper.

"I do," Amber snapped. "Is Uncle Michael coming over tonight?"

"I don't think so."

The lines in Amber's face became positively mutinous.

"Oh," she said loudly when Kevin emerged from the car. "Is he ever ugly."

"Amber!"

"Uggie," Tucker said, as if in agreement.

Amber glared at Kevin with naked dislike.

"If you are rude, Amber, I will have no choice but to send you to your room."

"Never mind," Amber said. "I'm going already."

She flounced away in a fine tiff, and slammed the door behind her.

Tucker, sensing aggravation in the air, tightened his hold on Sadie's leg.

"Uggie," he whispered.

"Hush, Tucker, don't say that again."

Trouble, Sadie thought. *I can just smell it coming. And if there's one thing a McGee has a good nose for, it's trouble.*

She looked at Kevin. He was at the trunk now taking luggage out. Quite a lot of luggage, considering he was only staying four days.

He wasn't ugly. Not by a long stretch. But she found herself thinking his appeal had paled somewhat.

Kevin was tall, and extremely blond. He had a fineness of bone that was revealed by the shape of his nose and his high cheekbones. His eyes were blue, full of keen intelligence.

He came toward her now, loaded down under about five thousand dollars' worth of fine luggage. He was wearing a suit. What kind of person spent a day driving in a suit?

Not the kind of person she could marry.

She should have never come back here.

She moved a step forward to greet him, but Tucker was holding on to her furiously.

Kevin set down the suitcases and smiled. Such a nice smile. Good grief, Sadie thought, Kate was right. I think he loves me. He leaned forward, like he was going to kiss her on the lips. She turned her cheek to him instead.

He regarded her thoughtfully for a moment, and if she was right, his smile was now tinged with a trace of sadness.

"Who is this?" he asked, peering behind her at Tucker, his voice full of that false hardiness of adults who don't deal well with children.

"Yuggie," Tucker said.

"Yuggie?" Kevin repeated, his face clearly indicating he thought he had hit the backwoods of America now. Where people had names like Bubba and Yuggie.

"This is my nephew Tucker."

"Tucker." Apparently he didn't consider that much of an improvement over Yuggie or Bubba. Kevin did have traces of snobbiness in him, and he was not good at hiding them.

Kevin stared. "Did you dress him?"

She held up her cast-encased hand. "He does the honor himself."

"I can tell," Kevin said. He was just joking of course, but Sadie could see how a stranger to him, like her brother, might think he was a bit pompous.

Today Tucker was wearing sweatpants with a pair of blue shorts over them. He also had a pair of striped shorts on his head.

Sadie thought it was adorable. Kevin didn't mean to be condescending. He was only making conversation. Why did she feel so uptight?

She detached Tucker from her pant leg. Silk. Silk with a little black handprint on it now.

What kind of person wore silk around the house in Sleepy Grove?

"Come in," she invited, opening the door.

He came in and set down his luggage inside the door. "My God," he said looking around. "What a beautiful home."

"Surprised to find it in Sleepy Grove, Idaho?"

"No," he said so quickly, he might as well have said yes. "And that's one of your brother's paintings."

He moved over to it. "Magnificent," he breathed.

Which was exactly what she had thought about Tucker's outfit.

Not that the painting wasn't magnificent, though it wasn't one of Sadie's favorites. To her it didn't have Mickey's usual vitality in it. It was of an empty garden swing underneath a tree.

It was full of sadness and Sadie could tell without asking it was one that had been done after Sam's illness.

"Your brother is very talented," Kevin said.

And you should hear what he thinks of you.

"Thank you."

"The other children?"

"The baby is sleeping. Amber is...around somewhere."

There. They seemed to have exhausted conversational opportunities between them.

They had never really had time together before. Not *days* of time. They were always dashing—running to get a quick bite to eat at lunch, hurrying to catch the opening credits of the movie, squeezing in dinner between work assignments.

Even those magnificent dinners weren't so much about being together as about wine selection and learning about forks.

"I'll show you your room." She took him down the hall to Sam and Mickey's room, feeling awkward, wishing he wasn't here, wishing she had never accepted the burden of his ring.

Wishing, mostly, that she had never come back here, to this place that shed such a different light on Kevin.

But mostly on herself.

He commented on how lovely the room was, and of course, it was. There was an en suite off the bedroom, and he spotted it.

"Would you mind terribly if I had a quick shower?"

"Not at all," she said.

If this was someone else, this conversation wouldn't be going like this. It would be full of breathless kisses, and exploring eyes and laughter coming out of nowhere.

The last thing on his mind would be a shower.

Unless it was an ice-cold one.

Now who was the mysterious *he* substituting for Kevin in her imaginary scenario?

She blushed.

They would have to sit down alone, soon. As soon as the children were in bed. She would have to tell him. Why did she feel so guilty? She had never told him yes in the first place. Only that she would think about it.

Maybe she felt guilty for that. Thinking about it, when she had known all along it couldn't be.

Kevin came out after his shower. Sadie had talked Amber into a game of Trouble to get her out of her room and hopefully out of her snit.

Considering what she could smell in the air with her famous McGee nose, it was probably a poor choice of game.

Kevin had changed into jeans and a sports shirt. The jeans had been pressed. His hair, just wet from the shower, did not have the same effect on her pulse as Michael's did.

"You must be Amber," he said.

Amber looked at him. Her brows drew down over her nose and she frowned. "Miss McGee to you."

He laughed.

Sadie glared at her niece. Amber pushed the bubble on the Trouble game with such fury it threatened to crack.

"The Old Man," Kevin said turning his attention to Sadie, "asked me to put some pressure on you about the proposal."

Everybody called Sadie's boss in Seattle the Old Man, though he couldn't have been much past forty.

She sighed, and looked at the kids. She tapped her cast lightly.

"That's why I'm here, your white knight to the rescue."

Amber rolled her eyes.

"In fact, I'm going to look after the kids for you while you go investigate the site. You need to take some pictures and things don't you?"

"*You're* going to baby-sit the kids?" Sadie asked incredulously.

"Sure. If you can do it, I can do it."

Sadie held up her broken hand. "There's more to it than you think."

"Yeah," Amber said under her breath. "There's more to it than you think."

"Sadie, I deal with high pressure. Do you really think there's anything about three little kids I can't handle?"

Amber was looking at him with a wicked gleam in her eye.

"It might not be such a good idea," Sadie said.

"But that's why I came," he insisted.

He was trying so hard to be nice. She had the unfortunate thought he might think he was going to win a few brownie points for this.

"No," she said.

"Nonsense. Get your camera and go. The Old Man asked me to bring your proposal back with me."

"Finished?" she yelped.

"I would think."

She felt a small stirring of panic. How was she going to pull that off in four days? Kevin was right. She needed to go see the site. She needed to do it now.

"All right. I'm going to leave you a neighbor's phone—" She stopped. What was she thinking? Leave him Michael's phone number in case anything went wrong? "I'll leave you my friend Kate's phone number in case you need it."

"Give me a break."

He didn't know what he was getting into. Oh well, in an hour he would be initiated. She jotted down Kate's phone number.

"Amber," Sadie said sternly to her niece, "be good."

"Oh, I will," Amber said with such sweet insincerity that Sadie almost decided to stay.

In the van headed for the old fire hall it struck her this was all wrong. Kevin had been there less than an hour and she was leaving to do work. Just like at home in Seattle. Work for both of them came first.

Now work seemed like a long way away. Light-years. As if it was intruding on her real life.

She shook away the thought impatiently.

She knew exactly where the fire hall was. It was not that far from her parent's home in the oldest part of Sleepy Grove. As children, she and Mickey had sometimes pulled the boards off one of the windows and wandered around inside, unmindful of such adult concerns as rotting timber. She wondered if the brass pole and the bell were there, both of which had given them so much enjoyment.

She pulled up in front of the old building and shook her head. It was an absolute mess. It had deteriorated quite a bit since the days she and Mickey had explored it. The wood was rotten, the windows were boarded or broken. Weeds grew chest high around it.

But the bell was still there, way up in the tower. The brass pole was probably salvageable, too.

Without getting out of the vehicle, she went through her briefcase and found her notes.

Gangway Productions wanted to tear this structure down and put a strip mall on the huge and mostly wasted lot the fire hall sat on. They wanted her company to come up with a proposal to make that palatable to the town.

She jotted down a few notes. This was going to be easy. If Kevin could keep the kids occupied for a few hours a day, she'd have this done in no time.

Firehouse Mall, she wrote in her little black notebook. In point form she began to make hasty notes: keep the flavor of history by saving the bell and brass pole; a bell tower could be reconstructed at the entrance of the mall, the brass pole used as part of a small outdoor play area for children.

She doubted her client was going to want to spend money on a small outdoor play area for children, but at this point the idea was just to get some things down on paper to show the client, ideas that would be very persuasive to the town council.

Sadie actually enjoyed this aspect of her work tremendously. Being creative. Letting the ideas flow. Stores, she continued writing, should have false fronts, giving the impression of a town from the Old West.

After writing for a few more minutes, she tucked her notepad into her purse and slung the bag over her shoulder. She took out the camera and got out of the van.

Though her hand was still in the cast, she had left off the sling this morning for the first time, and was finding things easier to manage. It was certainly going to help in taking pictures.

She walked around the building, fighting her way through weeds. She framed the building in her viewfinder.

Suddenly she became aware of the building, the soft sunshine wrapping it in golden light. It really was a rather lovely old place she thought, snapping the picture.

She was hit by a strange feeling of nostalgia, almost as if she could hear her and Mickey's voices from years ago.

"You look like you've seen a ghost."

She nearly jumped out of her skin. "Michael! What are you doing here?"

And why was she so damnably pleased to see him? After last time and that sizzling, seducing kiss they had shared, she should run the other way.

But her feet didn't seem to be doing any running.

"Looking. Same as you. It's beautiful, isn't it?"

It didn't seem like he was even thinking of that kiss. Well, why should he? He was probably kissed with a lot more regularity than she was.

"It's funny, I never thought so as a kid. Mickey and I used to play here. It just seemed like a falling-down old building. Now I can see it does have some charm and character. Too bad it's going to be torn down."

"It's not going to be torn down," Michael said. "Want to have a look inside?"

"It's probably all locked up—"

"There's some boards off a window in the back."

"No kidding," she said with a grin. "I think Mickey and I took those off a thousand years ago."

"Come on, let's have a peek."

Why not? It might be her last chance. Plus, there was

something about slipping into that old building with him that was irresistible. She slung her camera around her neck and followed him through the weeds to the back.

"I can't go in there." She wasn't a nimble ten-year-old anymore. Besides, she was still wearing her silk pants, and she was playing with only one arm.

"Sure you can. I'll help."

"My slacks—"

"They have to go to the cleaners anyway. Handprint." He leaned closer. "Tuck's. Where are the kids, anyway? They probably would have loved this."

"They're with Kevin," she said uncomfortably.

"When did he arrive?"

She didn't want to admit less than an hour ago, so she muttered something about earlier.

"And you're here sight-seeing alone?"

"I'm not exactly sight-seeing. I thought he should get to know the kids." That was misleading. Misleading him into thinking she was going to say yes to Kevin. Misleading him so he wouldn't even guess what her heart did every time he was near.

He stooped down by the window. "Okay, climb up on my shoulder and hop in."

She hesitated. More physical contact with him. Just what her raging hormones needed. Of course, it was innocent enough.

"I suppose I'm going to break my other arm," she said, but she took off her shoes and scrambled up on his shoulder. She could feel the taut, hard muscle underneath the fabric of his shirt. She knew she had better not linger. She was able to step easily through the window, collecting a few cobwebs on her slacks as she went.

She found she didn't care.

It was silly, but this felt fun. A small adventure. Did he

have a knack for turning ordinary things into the extraordinary?

Michael passed her shoes through to her, but she set them by the window and didn't put them back on. Uncomfortable things. The old floor felt smooth and cool under her feet.

He thumped down in the darkness beside her.

Her eyes were adjusting to the dimness.

"The pole's still here," she breathed.

"You going to try it?"

"With my arm?"

"You probably still could. I'll go first, just in case you get into trouble."

Suddenly, nothing could have kept her from the cool brass of the pole. They ran up the stairs together.

He went down first, then held himself, with easy strength, so that he was right below her. Using her upper arm instead of her hand, she latched on to the pole.

"Ready?"

He was right underneath her. This was most undignified. And she didn't care.

"You bet," she called.

Down they went. He caught her weight before she hit the ground.

"Too slow," she told him, turning in his arms. But her heart was beating as if she had scooted down that brass fireman's pole at the speed of light.

He stepped back from her instantly, smiling but with something smoky and mysterious in his eyes.

"That one was just for practice. Race you back to the top," he called, already running for the stairs.

"Whee," she cried, as she slid willy-nilly down the pole the second time. He didn't catch her this time. No sooner had her feet hit the ground than she was running back up the stairs. "I'll go alone this time," she insisted.

Was it memory that made this so fun? Or the rich spontaneity of the moment? Or him being with her? This dusty old place suddenly warm with its history, with his smile, with the delight of being impetuous.

She must have gone down the pole a dozen times with him following right behind her, before she collapsed laughing on the floor beneath it. The sunlight was streaming through the boards in the window and falling across the floor. Dust motes danced in sunbeams.

He collapsed beside her.

Companionable.

With a promise of a whole lot more.

"You're getting dust on your pants."

She wrinkled her nose at him. "As you pointed out, they needed dry-cleaning anyway."

"How's silk for sliding?"

"The best."

He leaned toward her, touched her neck. "Hey, you found it."

She felt herself color to the roots of her hair. "Oh. Yes. I forgot. I meant to give it to you."

She had meant to take it off. But somehow she hadn't. She had reached for it a few times. She had even undone the clasp. But she had never quite removed it. She liked the weight of it, felt a lovely warmth coming from the metal.

He didn't move his fingers. "I want you to have it."

She was startled. "But why?"

He shrugged. "I don't know for sure. A souvenir, maybe. Of your time in Sleepy Grove."

With him as her neighbor. Eating waffles in her bed, sliding down fire poles with her.

As if she was ever going to forget, anyway.

She should refuse. That would be the proper thing to do. But she couldn't. "Thank you," she said softly.

He dropped the weight of the chain. The light touch of his fingers left her neck. She would have mourned the loss of contact, except that his lips begged her to kiss them.

And so she did.

She leaned forward, impulsively, and kissed him.

His hand found its way to the back of her neck, and what she told herself she had meant only as a simple thank-you quickly became something else.

Lightning on dry grass.

"You've got to quit doing that to me, Sadie," he murmured thickly in her ear.

"What?" She sighed back.

"Kissing me. Lighting fires in me that nothing can put out. That keep me awake at night, thinking thoughts of you." He laughed, deep in his throat. "Sleepless in Sleepy Grove."

He was right. She had acted wantonly. She pulled away from him.

"I said the wrong thing, didn't I?"

"N-no," she stammered. "That was foolish. I'm sorry. I don't know what I was thinking." She was dusting off her silk pants frantically.

"I know what you were thinking," he said huskily. "Exactly."

"You don't!" she denied. "I was thinking what a terrible shame it is that this old building is going to be torn down."

It was a lie. She had been thinking no such thing. At least not in the last five minutes.

But his hand fell from her neck, and he looked at her with puzzled eyes.

"I told you it's not."

She reached into her purse and handed him her notebook.

He looked at it for a long time, reading her proposal, looking at her rough sketches.

"Aw, Sadie," he finally said.

"What? You don't like it?"

"I'm bidding on it. I'm going to restore it."

"It's falling down!"

"It's worth saving. There's a lot of history here."

She snorted, wanting to be relieved the kiss was behind them, wanting to be pleased that this wall was going up so swiftly between them.

But she ached for the moment that was lost, and would never come back. She did her best to keep that ache out of her voice. "Sleepy Grove history is not exactly the signing of the Declaration of Independence."

"Still paying back the town that snubbed you, Sadie? That *you* thought snubbed you?"

He said it so quietly. Maybe that's why it hurt so much, like a knife being put right in her heart.

He knew. The insecurity she tried so hard to hide, he knew about.

"Of course I'm not paying back the town! It's not personal."

"You're going to take a piece of the town's history and destroy it for no other reason than that's what you get paid to do? Pardon me if I take that a little personally."

"It's a falling-down piece of junk, and only a hopeless dreamer could ever believe he was going to save it."

"That's me," he said, looking at her in a way that made her heart break in two. "Hopeless dreamer. Feel the wood under your feet, Sadie? Solid oak."

"Big deal," she said defensively.

He looked at her. "The tough girl comes out now. I guess that's what I always forget about you, Sadie. You have this past you can't let go of. Maybe destroying some of the past of this little town you hate is going to help you out, but I doubt it."

"I don't hate it here," she said, still defensive. "I just don't like it. A little sleepy backwater isn't for everybody, you know."

"Yeah. Right. Just come back long enough to change the face of it forever. Give us a video arcade and an all-night convenience store. Then leave."

"I was always leaving," she said.

"I know." He stood up. "You're not getting it without a fight, you know. My proposal is better than that." He tossed her notebook back down at her.

"I've only spent five minutes on it. It's rough."

"It won't win."

"Well, now that you've had a good look at mine!"

"A little corporate espionage. You should be used to that type of thing in your fast-moving circles."

His voice was hard with cynicism.

She ached for the warmth of his laughter of a moment ago. She ached for the passion of his lips and the strength of his arms. She wouldn't let him know that if her legs were on fire.

"I'm just doing my job," she said coldly. "What do you want from me? Quit because you want the same piece of property as I do?"

He regarded her steadily. "You know, Sadie, I don't know what I want from you. I've never known. The funny thing is I don't think you know what you want from you, either."

"I do so."

The silence stretched between them. She could not think of one single thing she wanted from herself to fill that silence with.

"Goodbye, Sadie." He said it with cold, hard finality. He didn't offer to help her back out the window. He turned from her and strode away, leaned over, and in one athletic hop was out the window.

She sat for a long time in the smudgy darkness. Long after she had heard his car start up and leave. The very age, the solidness of the building, comforted her in some way she did not understand.

So she was stunned when she reached up and touched her cheek to find it wet with tears.

She drove back to Sam and Mickey's. She wouldn't call it home. Couldn't.

She could smell trouble before she was halfway up the walk. She broke into a run.

The baby was wailing, but other than that, the silence was unnerving.

She burst through the door. Kevin was sitting on the couch, his head back, a cold compress over his eyes.

"What?" she cried.

Without removing his compress, he fished in his pocket and held out his watch.

A Rolex, the crystal smashed.

"What happened?"

"She showed me a magic trick."

"Oh, no."

"Promised she could do it. Said she'd done it a hundred times. Rolled my watch in a handkerchief and proceeded to smash it with a hammer."

"I'm so sorry. Just give me a minute to check on the baby. I'll be right back."

She hurried up the hall into the boys' room. Tucker was under the bed. She scooped a tearstained Tyler from the crib. He continued to wail.

Amber crept in. "He needs his pants changed. Pom-Pom Donkey wouldn't do it."

"You promised you wouldn't call him that."

"I don't care," she said, her lip trembling. "He is mean and nasty."

"You wrecked his watch!"

"The trick didn't work the same as on TV."

"Do you know what that watch is worth?"

"He told me. Stupid to spend that kind of money on a watch. Stupid to give your watch to a little kid with a hammer."

She had a point there, Sadie thought. "He wanted you to like him," she said quietly. "That is why he trusted you with his watch. You have to apologize."

"I already did. He sent me to my room anyway."

"Good for him."

"Where's Uncle Michael?" she asked, her lip trembling violently, tears spilling out of huge eyes. "Why don't you like Uncle Michael better than that awful man? You could marry him. You could stay here and look after me if something happens to my—" A stricken look crossed her face.

"Honey," Sadie said softly, getting down on her knees. "I'll always be here for you. I don't have to marry anybody for that."

"Please don't marry that man," Amber whispered, creeping into her arms and sighing.

"I'm not going to," Sadie said. She braced herself for the next question. She thought Amber would ask her if she was going to marry Michael, but Amber didn't ask her that.

"Is my mom going to die?" she asked.

"Oh, honey, I don't think so."

"I want my mommy," Amber whispered brokenly. Her hot tears washed down Sadie's neck.

"Mommy," Tucker croaked, and came out from under

the bed. He climbed onto her extra knee and wrapped his arms around her, too. And cried, big, fat, heart-breaking baby tears.

Tyler's face was turning a most unbecoming shade of purple.

An exhausting hour later she had all the children calmed down and in bed. She made tea in the kitchen and brought some to Kevin.

He still had the compress over his eye. He took it off.

"What happened?" she said, staring at the black and blue around his eye.

"I was trying to hold the baby. He reared back and caught me with his head. I thought babies had soft heads."

"Oh, Kevin," she said softly. "What a mess."

She handed him the tea and then sat beside him. The silence stretched. She gave him the ring.

"I guess this is your answer, then?"

She nodded. "I'm sorry. I—"

"Don't say sorry. I'm the one who is sorry. We probably could have gone on indefinitely if I hadn't pushed this on you. Now I've gone and changed everything."

Everything had gone and changed, all right, but she didn't know how much Kevin had to do with it, or if it was just the universe moving into the order of its own design.

"Kevin, I like you, and we've had some good times together. But I don't think I love you."

"I knew."

"Then why would you—"

"Who knows? Hope shines eternal, I suppose."

"Did you love me, Kevin?"

"I do love you, Sadie."

"You never said anything!"

"No. You get mad at the gushy parts during movies. You make faces at couples who hold hands in public. That's why I thought maybe it didn't matter if you didn't love me back. I thought you just didn't believe in it. You know, a sweet old-fashioned idea that you had outgrown.''

"I don't believe in it. Didn't," she amended.

"Didn't?" His eyebrows shot up. "Meaning you do—"

"Oh, you know, kids. They can make believers out of anyone."

"That's not quite the effect they had on me."

"I'm sorry. They just don't take to strangers that readily. Tuck spent the first few days I was here, under the bed, and I'm his aunt."

"It was the little girl who seemed to take a dislike to me."

"Amber is going through an awful lot for a small child. You'll have to forgive her. She's mixed-up right now."

A McGee trait.

"I know. I'm so sorry about her mother. Have you heard anything further?"

"She has a cousin in New York they're going to try for a match."

He rolled the ring in his fingers and then quickly tucked it into his pocket and picked up his tea.

"I knew a woman like you would never marry a man like me," he said.

"What do you mean *a woman like me?*" she asked, and braced herself for his answer. Here it comes. Wrong side of the tracks. Ill-bred. Uses the wrong fork.

"You know," he said. "A woman so full of life, so vibrant, so very…alive."

Her mouth fell open. "What ever makes you think I'm like that?"

He laughed softly. "The sparkle in your eyes. The joy in your laugh. The goodness in your heart. Sadie, it always made me laugh inside that you thought it mattered wha you wore, or what fork you used, when what you are just shines through. All the trappings dim in comparison to what you are.''

He had loved her. Did. She felt embarrassed and honored and sad.

"Don't you waste one minute feeling sad, Sadie," he said gently, reading her mind. "I'll get over it."

With the first hint of mischief she'd ever seen in him, he pulled out a paper and flashed it in front of her.

In big dark bold letters it said WENDA, followed by a phone number.

"Where on earth did you meet her?"

"She brought by a casserole a while ago. And made me up the cold compress while she was here."

Sadie laughed. He laughed with her. She thought maybe it was the first time they had laughed together.

The phone rang. The laughter still ringing in her voice, she picked it up.

"Sadie, it's Michael." His voice was hard and cold as an Arctic wind.

Even so, she had thought that last goodbye had the awful ring of finality to it. If he was calling, something was wrong.

"What is it?" she asked with trepidation.

"I've just had a phone call from a man who lost a pony. I think Pom-Pom is probably his."

Chapter Nine

Michael slammed down the telephone receiver. She'd sounded so happy when she answered the phone. Well, why not? Her boyfriend—almost fiancé—was there. Together they were probably cheerfully plotting the destruction of any building in town over twenty years old.

He looked at the mess on his kitchen counter.

What was he doing baking bread? Had he completely lost his marbles?

Yes, a little voice answered him. *Completely.*

Somewhere in that bread book it said he got to punch that stuff rising out of the bowl like some awful ooze from a horror movie.

Putting the full weight of his fury and frustration behind it, he punched the dough. And punched it and punched it and punched it.

He punched it until his arms ached and his heart didn't. Almost.

He wandered casually over to his kitchen window and took a look out. For the ninth time, but who was counting?

The lights were still on over there. That big, sleek car sat outside, shining like silver in the moonlight.

He was suddenly very aware his pickup was twelve years old and in need of paint.

"But I like my pickup," he announced to himself. He'd even named it. John Henry.

She'd done well for herself. She was going to marry a rich lawyer with a big car. They were going to live in a mansion in Seattle and have maids to raise their children.

If they ever found a break in their busy schedules to discuss the possibility of children.

"She couldn't keep her hands off me," he muttered to himself. "What's she doing over there with *him?*"

He probably shouldn't have walked out of the fire hall in a huff, because the way things had been developing, Mr. Block-long car would have been sent packing before he had time to properly unpack.

What had made him so mad? The fact that the sweetness of her lips was hiding some hard part of her soul?

He wished he could make himself believe that.

She was spoken for. That's why he'd left her before things got too far out of hand. Wasn't it?

Why was he so full of regret now, the remembered taste of her lips nearly driving him mad?

He turned his back on the window, went back to the bowl and gave the contents of it a few more hard jams with his balled-up fists. Madness.

He picked the gluey substance out of the bowl. Okay, so maybe his punching had been a little too energetic. He was not an expert, but this bread looked like it had been KO'd. He'd lost interest in bread making anyway. He put the gummy pancake in the garbage, then looked with distaste where bits of bread dough stuck to his fingers.

Another excuse to head over to his kitchen window,

which was right above the sink. He opened the tap and ran water over his hands. He looked at the clock. It was getting late.

The living room light at her house winked out.

Her bedroom light came on.

He waited, holding his breath. Sure enough, on the other side of the house, a ribbon of light appeared along the grass.

They weren't sharing a bedroom.

He began to breathe again.

Not, he told himself, scrubbing furiously at his hands, that it was any of his business.

Not, he told himself, that he cared.

He went back to his kitchen counter with a dishcloth and discovered something he never knew about bread. Chunks of dough stuck to the counter in an uncooked state hardened into cement. To get this off, he was going to need the scraper he used to get ice off his truck windows in the wintertime.

The man who had called about the pony had sounded very old. He said he'd heard about it on the radio. He lived close to Bonner's Ferry, Idaho. How did a pony manage to wander sixty-two miles from home? More interesting, why would a pony wander sixty-two miles from home?

Horses, even small ones, were creatures of habit. They didn't like leaving their homes, their yards, everything that was familiar.

Perhaps—and he resisted an impulse to cross his fingers—it was not the same pony.

Michael sighed and gave up on the mess. Forget the window scraper. It was going to take a jackhammer to get the cementlike substance off his countertop.

But if that pony had traveled that distance, that would explain why he had looked so terrible. Possibly not because he'd been neglected or abused, but because he'd been traveling, eating what he could find, scrounging. Getting filthier every day. How long had it taken him to find his way to the garden in Sleepy Grove?

Michael went and sat in his living room, such as it was. He tried to see it through Sadie's eyes, since he'd asked her to come over here in the morning. Almost every available space was covered in red wooden fire trucks at some stage of assembly. His workbench, that he'd built specially so he could stand at it without hurting his back, was in the center of the room. The trucks he'd starting building for Amber and Tucker were there, in pieces.

Destined-to-be-lady-of-the-manor Sadie would probably get a real laugh out of this. He'd always liked making her laugh before. Why was he scowling so hard, his forehead hurt?

Because of Amber, he told himself. Amber was attached to the pony now. Just like Sadie had said she was going to be. Sadie was going to be furious with him if the man who had called was the pony's rightful owner.

And well she should be. He had probably made a mistake. A big one that involved a little girl's heart. He could buy her another pony but he knew it wouldn't be the same.

"Aw, hell, O'Bryan," he said to himself. "Why do you have to screw up so royally when you do?"

Sadie arrived at his door promptly at ten. He'd told her to come here to meet the man claiming ownership to Pom-Pom.

"We don't know anything about the man," Michael had said on the phone last night. "I wasn't going to give him your address."

"Kevin's here. I would have been all right."

"I didn't give him your address because he might have come and cased out the pony."

"Oh." Of course he wasn't concerned for her well-being, Sadie thought. Why should he be?

She didn't think aging ponies were exactly prime targets for unscrupulous con men, but she'd refrained from saying so. The edge of anger in his voice was too close to the surface.

Now she stood on his step, he looking down at her, she feeling an ache for the warmth that was missing from his eyes.

He looked tired. She wanted to reach up and touch his face in greeting. Instead, she stuffed her hands deep into her jacket pocket.

"You don't look like you slept well," she ventured.

Maybe they should reopen the subject of the fire hall. Maybe if she explained to him—

"I was worried about Amber."

"Oh." Ridiculous to think he'd been awake thinking of their parting of ways over the fire hall.

"Come in."

She had never been in his house. She wondered what it would tell her of him? Would there be deep black leather sofas and a sophisticated stereo system? Lights that dimmed?

No, he liked old things. She remembered the pictures of the house he'd renovated that had appeared in *Heritage*. His place would probably have more the look of a hunting lodge. Big masculine furniture, old rifles and snowshoes on the walls.

She stepped in, and stopped. Her mouth fell open.

No swinging bachelor pad, and no country-inn look, either.

"Is this Santa's workshop?"

"A hobby," he said curtly.

But she knew it wasn't. It was something more; each of

these exquisite fire trucks was an expression of something deeply creative inside of him.

There was one humble-looking couch in the room, an old stereo, an even older television. It looked like it might even be black-and-white.

And then there were trucks everywhere. On bookcases and overturned boxes, on shelves, on the arms of the couch, on top of the TV. Hook-and-ladder trucks, pumper trucks, old-fashioned trucks and newfangled trucks. Red. Fire engine red, every single one of them.

"You don't mind if I look, do you? Until he gets here?"

Michael shook his head, but there was nothing inviting in his eyes.

As she looked at the trucks and the care that had gone into making each one of them, she suddenly knew how much the fire hall meant to him, how deep her betrayal must seem to him. Even if it was unintentional. Even if it was a strange coincidence that had brought them both to be interested in the same property at the same time, for very different reasons.

"What do these have to do with the fire hall?" she asked quietly. She picked up one of the trucks. It was sanded so smooth, it felt like silk where her fingertips touched it.

"I'm going to move my workshop there, and have a small storefront, though most of my business is mail-order."

"It's an awfully big space."

"A friend wants to use part of it for a restaurant."

She knew it was a woman. She felt a stab of jealousy. She wanted to ask who. Instead, she asked, "Could I buy one of these? For Tucker?"

"No."

Just like that. He was giving no pieces of his heart into her keeping. And perhaps it was just as well. Because if she bought one of these trucks, lovingly crafted by Michael's hand, could she ever part with it?

"They're spoken for. These are all preordered for Christmas."

So, it was nothing personal. It still felt personal.

It felt like he was saying, *Remember? We're on different sides of the fence. Let's not pretend anything else.*

"Come into the kitchen. We'll have a coffee. Where are the kids?"

"With Kevin. I really can't stay long. If he doesn't come soon—"

"The kids hate Kevin," he guessed softly, and with just a trace of satisfaction.

"Of course they don't *hate* him."

"Ah. Dislike him intensely?"

"Closer," she said wryly. He actually smiled at her.

He led her through to his kitchen. A few fire trucks had even found their way in here. There was one tucked behind the phone book on the counter, and another on top of the fridge.

The kitchen was lovely—the cabinets brand-new, raised panel golden oak, the floors ceramic tile, an old red brick chimney forming a charming visual focal point for the entire room.

"Did you renovate this?"

He nodded, his back to her as he got down mugs. She sat at the stool at his kitchen counter. She picked thoughtfully at some of the hardened-on white substance.

"Glue?" she guessed.

"Close," he said and handed her her coffee. He put a five-pound bag of sugar and a carton of milk on the counter and handed her a spoon.

She could tell he'd been a bachelor for a good long time.

He probably couldn't change now even if someone wanted to have him. Which she didn't, of course.

His kitchen smelled good. Of what? Coffee, rich and aromatic. But something else.

The doorbell rang.

Not yeast?

"Sadie, I'm sorry. If this pony belongs to this man—"

"No," she said firmly. "You were always right about the pony. It came because it was meant to. If it goes..." Her voice trailed away. He gave her a look and then went to the door.

When he came back, Sadie's heart fell. He was accompanied by a little old man in a plaid shirt with patches on the elbows and baggy wool pants held up with ancient suspenders. His white hair grew in funny little tufts, like spun cotton candy. Blue eyes twinkled from a bed of wrinkles.

"Fernando Martinez," the old man said, extending a hand. His grip was surprisingly strong and sure.

Not the kind of man who was trying to work some kind of con to get a free pony.

Her eyes met Michael's. He knew. She knew. This was the pony's owner.

"Let's go," she said, getting up off her stool. "I'll show you where your pony is, Mr. Martinez."

"The coffee smells good," he said hopefully.

Sadie sank back on her stool. She just wanted to get this over with. But Michael poured the old man a steaming cup of brew.

"Delicious," he said, taking a deep sip. "Angelo can wait a few more minutes. It's been a long time since I had such good coffee."

"Is that what you call him? Angelo?" Sadie asked.

"Angelo, yes. Are you married?" he asked Sadie boldly.

"N-n-nooo," she stammered.

"Then marry him." He wagged his eyebrows in Michael's direction. "I'd marry him myself for coffee like this."

"She's engaged," Michael told his guest. "Not to me."

She could have corrected him. She wasn't engaged. She never *officially* had been. But she wasn't going to get into that right now in front of a complete stranger. Who had just suggested she marry Michael. It might look like she was considering it.

"Ah." The man looked from one to the other.

"How long has Angelo been missing?" Michael asked, not looking at Sadie.

He did make delicious coffee, she thought.

"A month. I didn't know where he could have gone. I have been sick with worry for him."

Out of the corner of her eye she saw the flicker of hope go out of Michael's eyes. He, too, had been hoping that the man had no attachment to the pony, that he would be willing to sell him.

"He played an important role in my family," the old man said softly. "Would you like to hear his story?"

She should just want to go home. But she liked it here in Michael's kitchen, sipping good coffee. And she liked this little old man.

Maybe she was just delaying the moment of truth, but she said yes, she wanted to hear Angelo's story.

"My beautiful daughter Maria had a beautiful daughter named Carina. When Carina, my granddaughter, was nine, she became very very ill. The doctors thought she would die.

"Maria brought her home, to me, to our house in the country, where Carina could look out the window and smell the country air, and see beautiful things, birds and flowers, cows in the field. Sometimes, even deer would come into the yard.

"One day, shortly after Carina had come, I saw Angelo at a little auction. He was very young and handsome then. I thought, I will bring him home and Carina will have something else to look at out her bedroom window.

"So I brought him home. I put him on the lawn right outside her window. He wandered around the whole yard. He ate everything in sight. He made a mess everywhere. He trampled the vegetables and ate the flowers.

"But none of that mattered. Because in my granddaughter's eyes a light came on. The light of life. Soon she began to smile. It was not long before Angelo was so bold that he was putting his head in her window and eating the flowers off her windowsill."

Sadie laughed. "He still does that."

Mr. Martinez nodded. "Carina laughed just the way you just did. A laugh that lit up everything around her, and especially my old heart.

"In another week or two, she was up at that window, and she told me she was going to get well so that she could ride Angelo. And a miracle happened. My granddaughter got stronger every day.

"One day she was strong enough to go outside and sit on the pony's back. Just a few seconds and she was tired, but the next day it was a few seconds longer. Soon she was able to ride him around the yard. And then one day, she was strong enough to take him out of the yard.

"She never looked back. Carina and Angelo went everywhere together. All up and down our country roads you'd see them, galloping along, her hair blowing in the wind, her cheeks full of healthy color, her legs and arms growing strong from clinging to that pony. She was like a girl who had never been sick.

"The pony gave my granddaughter back her life. I do not know how it is so, only that it is, and that he is so special to me. My granddaughter is gone now—" he read both their horrified expressions and laughed. "Not gone like that, grown-up gone. Perhaps you have heard of her? Catina Martinez, member of the United States Olympic Equestrian Team?" He beamed with pleasure and with pride.

"Anyway, she comes to see her old friend Angelo and her old grandpa not so much anymore. He is very old now, my Angelo. Nearly thirty. And I am very old now, too. Both of us a little lonely, I think."

Sadie got up quickly wiping a sleeve across her eyes. "We better go and see him."

Michael gathered up the coffee things, but unless she was mistaken, a sleeve was wiped quickly across his eyes while he had his back to them, too.

The little old man took one of her arms and one of Michael's and they walked him across the street. He moved so slowly.

Kevin was out loading his suitcases in his car. Tucker was jumping up and down on one of them.

"I thought he was staying a few days," Michael commented.

"He's had a change of plan."

Michael was looking at her *hard*. She made her face into a cool mask.

They went through the side gate into the yard and down to their little makeshift horse paddock. Angelo looked up from his feeding frenzy, nickered softly and went back to eating.

Mr. Martinez went into the pen and touched the pony with gentle, gnarled hands. Then he laid a wrinkled cheek against Angelo's shaggy shoulder. "Ah, Angelo," he said.

"You are so handsome again. Someone young and strong to brush you and spoil you?"

Sadie watched with growing sadness. Hadn't she suspected for some time that such a gentle soul as Pom-Pom—Angelo—could not have known abuse?

Amber suddenly came tumbling out of the house.

"Who are you?" she demanded of Mr. Martinez. "What are you doing to *my* pony?"

"Are you the one who has been brushing my Angelo every day?" Mr. Martinez asked her gently.

"His name isn't Angelo. It isn't! It's Pom-Pom. He's not your pony."

"Amber—" Sadie said.

Amber's looked from face to face and read the truth there. Her eyes filled up with tears. Turning, she ran back toward the house.

The man looked after her, his face soft. "So, Angelo has found himself another little girl to help heal."

"I'm sorry," Sadie said. "She was unforgivably rude. She's become very attached to the pony."

"Her heart is heavy?" Mr. Martinez pressed perceptively.

Sadie sighed and nodded. "Her mother is very ill right now, and Angelo has provided a distraction for her."

"Ah." The old man nodded. "I am beginning to understand. Why, I ask myself, would my fat little pony leave his home and all his comforts? Why did he travel so far? Why would he come to stop here? Why did no one find him along the way?"

"I asked myself the same questions," Michael said.

"I think Angelo knew he had one last mission before his time here was done and he can return to his home with angels," the old man said. "I always thought of him that way. A small angel. A messenger from heaven."

"We can't take your pony, Mr. Martinez," Sadie said gently. What a fanciful old man. She could not take his only friend from him.

"He is not my pony anymore," Mr. Martinez answered her. "I am old now. You see how slowly I move. Even feeding a small pony is very hard for me. But I promised him, a long time ago, when he helped Carina get well that he would always have a home. And I will not have broken my promise if I give him to that little girl. He belongs now to that little one. I am happy knowing he is safe. I am happy knowing he once again has a sense of purpose. A job to do."

Sadie looked at Michael for guidance. Could she accept this generous gift? For Amber? He nodded, a small smile on his lips. He didn't even look angry at her anymore.

"Sadie." Kevin came out the back door and walked toward them. When he arrived, she made introductions.

"Oh, Kevin, this is Mr. Martinez, the man who owns the pony." She smiled. "Used to own the pony. And this is my neighbor, Michael."

"Ah, this is the neighbor," Kevin said, and extended his hand. "Your brother's on the phone, Sadie. It seemed it might be urgent."

She did not want to leave these two men in each other's company for any length of time, especially with them eyeing each other up and down with such keen appraisal. But what could she do? Giving them an apprehensive glance, she turned and went to the house.

"Mickey?"

She felt her heart growing wings at his words.

"Really?" She began to cry. Amber came and stood silently inside the kitchen door, staring at her. She gave her a watery smile. "Amber," she said, "your mom's going to be fine."

Amber looked at her woodenly. She didn't quite understand. In a minute she would get Mickey to explain it all to her.

"You'll ask Mrs. Height to baby-sit for a few more weeks? No, you won't."

She knew she couldn't do this. She had her job to consider. Commitments.

And she knew she'd made a promise to her niece. She had promised her she would be there if she needed her.

And she needed her right now.

"I'll stay on as long as you need me."

Amber turned and slipped away.

"Amber," Sadie called, "just wait a minute. Your daddy wants to talk to you." But Amber didn't come back.

"I'll get her to call you back, Mickey. She's upset right now. A man showed up who owned the pony. Well, don't be glad too quickly. He said she could have it, but I haven't told her yet. What kind of person gives away a pony? You would have to meet him to believe it. Don't worry, Mickey, the pony hardly takes up any space at all, and he's only eaten one of your paintings. Just kidding. My love to Sam."

She hung up the phone.

"Amber," she called. "Where are you?"

Her voice echoed emptily back at her. She went back outside. Perhaps she'd gone back to the pony.

Kevin and Michael were chatting away like the best buddies in the world, which made the hair stand right up at the back of her neck.

"Is Amber out here?"

The men all shrugged. Michael looked at her closely.

"Sadie?" He was suddenly right in front of her, looking down. He caught her shoulders in his grasp.

She began to cry.

"What's happened?" he asked with gentle concern.

"I'm being silly," she managed to choke out. "Every thing's fine. They've—" her voice abandoned her again for a minute "— they've found a match. A perfect match. Sam is going to get a kidney."

"Really?" Michael breathed. And then she was in his arms, laughing and crying. He picked her up by the waist and twirled her around in a mad and ecstatic celebration.

Finally he set her down, breathless. She blushed when she saw Kevin and Mr. Martinez staring at them, their mouths open.

"Which of you is she marrying?" Mr. Martinez asked with confusion.

Michael stepped away from her so abruptly, she nearly fell over. "Him," he growled.

Kevin's eyebrows shot up. "Me? I'm afraid not. Not that I didn't try."

Michael was looking askance at her. Mr. Martinez was smiling with a look of wise knowing. Kevin was looking from her to Michael with amusement.

"Where are the kids?" she asked. "I have to tell the kids."

Michael took her hand. "Yeah, let's find the kids. I can't wait to see the look on Amber's face."

His hand around hers felt so good. Like this was how she should face life. All its good moments and all its bad ones, too. With her hand in Michael's.

Of course it was impossible.

But that didn't mean she was going to cut this magic moment short. No, she was going to enjoy it for as long as it lasted.

"Amber," she called.

"Amber," Michael called.

After a long hunt, they found her hidden in a pocket inside a hedge.

She was crying silently, huge teardrops leaving a trail of white down her grimy face.

It was Michael who braved the thorny tree, and went in after her.

"Come here, sweetie."

He pulled her onto his lap, tucked her head against his shoulder and let her cry.

"Is my mom going to die?" she sobbed. "Is she? I saw Auntie Angel crying, talking to my dad on the phone. I saw her. What will I do if my mommy dies? What will I do?"

"Shhh, sweetie," Michael said so gently, holding her tight to him. "Shhh. Auntie Angel was crying happy tears. Grown-ups do that sometimes. You know what? Your mommy's going to get a brand-new kidney, and I think she's going to be just fine."

Taking a deep breath, Sadie braved the prickly tree and pushed her way into the little hollow. There was hardly any room.

It was wonderful. Her and Amber and Michael all pressed together in the sanctuary of the shrub, sharing this moment.

Amber stopped crying and looked at him soberly, and then at Sadie. "Don't lie to me," she whispered. "Sometimes people lie to little kids to make them feel better, but it doesn't make me feel any better."

"Amber, I swear I will never, ever lie to you."

She sighed contentedly. "My mom's getting a kidney?"

"Yeah," Michael told her gently.

Amber reached out and took Sadie's hand and pressed herself deeper into Michael's shoulder.

"It's okay then," she said bravely, "about Pom-Pom. That was the deal I made."

"The deal you made?" Sadie prodded her.

"With God. I told him if my mommy could live, I didn't need anything else, not even the pony."

Michael and Sadie exchanged glances over her head.

"Well, honey," Michael said softly, "I think maybe God has a soft spot for little girls. Come on. You need to talk to Mr. Martinez."

He crawled out from the bushes with Amber, and with easy strength lifted her onto his shoulders.

Sadie walked beside them, feeling like a ring of bright light was around them, shimmering with love and with hope.

She wanted to reach out and take his hand again. She wanted the warmth of his hand in hers to make this moment perfect.

He would probably still be mad about the fire hall when the excitement had died down.

She would still have to go someday.

Still, life didn't offer so many perfect moments.

It would be foolish to not take one that was offered to her. She slipped her hand into his.

He smiled down at her.

For one perfect, shining moment, she believed everything could be all right.

Maybe, just maybe, God had a soft spot for big girls, too.

Chapter Ten

Sadie hung up the phone. Her ear actually ached, she had been on the phone so much tonight.

She went and checked on the children. All fast asleep, Amber's lips still inches from the picture of her mom that she so often fell asleep holding.

Sadie pried it from her grasp and set it back on the dressing table. She looked at her niece for a long time—the soft, thick loops of hair, the round, pink cheeks, the sweep of thick lashes.

She had done the right thing. The only thing.

It was just that she hadn't known the price when she had decided what to do.

And now that she did know the price, she wouldn't change her mind anyway.

Closing the door on Amber, she paced restlessly around the house, then finally put on a sweater and went out into the yard. The fall night was cool and crisp. The sky was clear and a million stars seemed to wink at her. She walked down toward Angelo. He didn't even glance up at her as she approached. She could hear him crunching his hay.

She smiled to herself. See? If she had stayed in Seattle she would have never learned this interesting fact. Never been still enough to know that ponies crunch hay.

She had never noticed the stars shining like this in Seattle, either.

"Hi, there."

She didn't even start when Michael appeared out of the shadows. "Hi," she said softly.

"What are you doing out here?"

She shrugged, and smiled. "You know. Sleepless in Sleepy Grove."

"Yeah, I know that one. What's bothering you?"

"What makes you think anything is bothering me?"

"I just know, Sadie. A little sag in your shoulders, a little furrow in your brow, a little cloud in eyes that are usually sky blue."

She sighed. How had this happened? How had this man come to know her so well in such a short period? Why did it feel so wonderful to have someone care enough about you to notice the little things?

"I just talked to my boss about staying on until Sam's on her feet. Amber, the kids, are just getting used to me. I don't want them to have to change again. I mean I know they love their grandma, but she'd want them to go stay at her house and it's just one more thing to disrupt their lives."

"What did your boss say?"

"To get my priorities straight. Funny, they already felt pretty straight to me."

"So, are you out of a job?"

"He wants me to think about it for a few days, but basically I'm out of a job. I don't need to think about it. I know the right thing to do. What *feels* right.''

"I could help you out, Sadie. If you want to go back, I'll figure out something for the kids. They're used to me. It wouldn't disrupt them too much.''

"You'd do that for me, Michael?'' She was touched, and yet saddened, too.

"For you. For them, too, I guess.''

"I thought, maybe, you wanted me to stay here.''

"I want you to do what makes you happy.''

She looked into his clear eyes. Was she kidding herself about what she saw there?

"You want to hear something funny, Michael? I don't really want to go back to Seattle. Coming back here has made me aware of some dissatisfactions I had with the job. I'm not sure I want to work somewhere where money is always the first consideration.''

Coming back here had made her aware of some personal dissatisfactions, too, like a deep and abiding loneliness, but she didn't want to get into that.

Instead, she said, "I don't know if this town has changed, or if I have, but I kind of like it here. I think I'll stay. I read in the paper tonight the Chamber of Commerce is looking for a public relations manager. Isn't there a kind of rough justice in that? That I could end up promoting Sleepy Grove?''

"You're staying, Sadie?''

"Yeah. You couldn't look after the kids anyway. Not with the firehouse coming up.''

"Maybe,'' he reminded her.

"I don't know. I talked to David Millhouse tonight, too.''

"Who?''

"He's the president of Gangway Productions.''

"Oh. The company that wants to mow down the fire hall."

"I had to be straight with him. I told him I was leaving the project, but that a local guy with a pretty solid reputation for historical renovations was competing for the site, and that I thought the town would go with you."

"You didn't have to do that."

"No, I didn't. But I felt I owed the truth to the client. There's no doubt in my mind the town will go with you. He had an interesting idea, though."

"Which was?"

"He asked if I thought you might go for a compromise. You restore the fire hall, and it becomes the anchor building for the rest of the mall."

"Well, well."

"The old and the new together, side by side. He said he'd call you."

"What's his interest in Sleepy Grove, anyway?"

"I asked him that. He's got two kids. The oldest one is starting school next year. He's had it with big cities. He and his wife are looking for something else. A quieter way of life. A place with a sense of community. I guess they came through here on holidays last year and fell in love with it."

"That happens to lots of people, Sadie."

"It does have a way of growing on you," she said quietly, then laughed. "Of course, so does fungus. Just kidding. You know, when I'm ready to raise a family, this is the kind of place I want to do it in, too."

His silence made her uneasy, so she kept talking. "You know, Mickey asked me to call my dad tonight, let him know the good news about Samantha."

"And?"

"What can I say? That he isn't what I am? Maybe I'm

even a better person for growing up the way I did. Stronger. More resourceful. More creative. Anyway, he was genuinely very happy about Sam.

"You know, Kate said I had to come back here. I thought she was wrong, but now I see she wasn't. She was right. You see, if I came back here and went right back to feeling like that girl from the wrong side of the tracks, then I'd never be free. I might cover it up with all kinds of things—clothes and cars and jewels and jobs—but that self-doubt would have always been there deep inside of me, making me try and prove myself over and over. That I belonged.

"Right now, it's the oddest thing, but right now I feel like I belong everywhere. Here. Seattle. It doesn't seem to make any difference.

"It's not important. Sam's getting to live. Now that's important."

Michael was looking at her so intently, she felt uncomfortable, rattling away like an idiot. Still, once started she couldn't seem to stop, especially since he didn't seem inclined to take up any of the slack.

She looked at the pony. "Angels come in every shape and size, don't they?"

He moved closer to her. His eyes never left her face. "Yeah," he said, "they do."

She laughed. "Don't look at me like that. I'm no angel."

"Your niece thinks you are."

"Well, kids, you know."

"And I dreamt you were an angel once. I told you, remember?"

"You didn't dream that."

He was silent.

"I came. When I heard you were hurt, I came."

"Why?" he asked softly.

She looked away from him, up at that huge sky full of stars. "Because I couldn't stay away."

"So why did you go?" His hand had come to rest on her shoulder.

"You had a girlfriend."

He sighed. "I guess I did, didn't I?"

"What happened to her?"

"I guess at some point she probably wanted more than I did."

"And what did you want?"

"I think it was you."

She was silent, though it seemed her heart was beating loudly inside her chest. She laughed nervously.

"I wasn't kidding."

She didn't know what to say. She slipped through the fence and ran her hands through Angelo's shaggy coat.

Michael came through the fence right behind her.

"You spoiled every other woman for me. None of them made me laugh like you did. Or feel so alive. Almost on fire with life."

She turned to him, her eyes wide. She searched his face. She felt her throat closing at what she saw there. No, she was not kidding herself.

"Me? Sadie McGee?"

"Yeah. You. Sadie McGee."

He loved her.

He was so close. He leaned yet closer.

He kissed her, his mouth meeting hers tenderly, with welcome, saying again what his eyes were saying.

He kissed her until her heart pounded and her breath was ragged and her thoughts a jumble of hope and passion.

The pony grunted approvingly.

She pulled away from Michael and touched her lips. It

was the moonlight. And Sam's wonderful news. It was this magical little messenger behind them.

She looked at his face.

No. It was more. It was a man and a woman who were meant to be together.

"Michael," she whispered.

"Auntie Angel." A wail came from the house.

"Amber doesn't sleep well when she's overly excited. I have to go."

"Angel duty," he said with wry regret. "I understand."

"Come with me?"

He shook his head. "Not if I want to keep the devil in me under control."

"And do you?" she teased boldly, moving away from him across the yard.

"I want it to be right between you and I, Sadie. No shortcuts."

Her tears nearly blinded her. He said that as if she was the kind of girl he was going to take home to meet his mother. The kind of girl who wore white at her wedding. The kind of girl he wasn't going to give in to temporary temptations with.

He said that as if she were a forever kind of girl.

"I'll send the kids to Kate's tomorrow afternoon," she called to him from the back door, her voice shaking. "Come then."

In the moonlight, she saw him salute her before she closed the door behind herself and went to Amber.

Good grief, he was going to be here any minute, and she'd made an utter mess of everything.

She'd learned something, though.

Never try to make jam with one hand out of commission.

Never try to make jam in good clothes.

Maybe never try to make jam, period.

The kitchen looked like a giant raspberry had come through the door and exploded. There were red splotches and sticky spots everywhere.

Only the bread, fresh from the bakery this morning, looked perfect. She looked closer. No, it had splotches on it, too.

The phone rang and she glared at it, wondering how to answer it. Finally she picked it up.

"Oh, hi, Kate." She cradled the receiver under her chin where she was pretty sure there was a clean spot. "Amber said she's allowed to go swimming? At this time of year? No! That's what you thought? Be very careful not to give her your watch.

"Kate, just since I have you on the phone, do you…well, this is silly, but do you by any chance know anything about jam?

"You do? The microwave? Eight minutes? Are you joking? Kate, I absolutely love you. Will you come to my wedding? What wedding? Well, I wasn't talking about a specific wedding. I just meant when I do get married, someday, you know, would you like to come?"

She hung up the phone, nearly dancing. She scooped a cup and three quarters out of her supply of raspberries and mashed them with the potato masher. She added three quarters of a cup of white sugar and a teaspoon of lemon juice.

"It can't be that easy," she thought, and debated calling Kate back. No, Kate already thought she was nuts.

She put the mix in a bowl and into the microwave.

Two minutes on high. Turn. Stir.

She groaned. That was not jam.

Two more minutes. Turn. Stir.

It still didn't look like jam, but the room was starting to smell kind of right.

Two minutes. Stir.

The room smelled heavenly. The mixture was actually starting to thicken.

Two minutes. Done. She took it out of the microwave. Aromatic steam rose off it. She let it cool, then finally, holding her breath, she stuck her finger in. And licked it.

"Jam!"

She actually had a sterilized jar to pour it into. She let it cool down, then put it in the fridge.

A knock came on the back door.

"Just a sec." She was going to scramble for the bathroom and wash some of the splotches off, do something with hair that had been steamed every which way.

The door squeaked open.

He came in.

She froze, looking at him.

To have him forever. Walking in the back door with that sweet smile on his face.

A smile that said what her heart knew, and her mind was still struggling to believe.

He didn't care if her hair was every which way.

He had something behind his back.

She felt herself growing red. Roses?

He held it out.

A paper. She took it. An application form from the Sleepy Grove Chamber of Commerce.

He wanted her to stay here.

There was something else behind his back. A ring?

Better.

Bread.

A little round loaf, that looked hard as a rock and rather dark in places.

"What a coincidence," she said, "when I just made—"

He looked around the room. He came up to her and touched her cheek, then he licked his finger.

"Jam?" he guessed.

She nodded.

It was ridiculous to be crying. But she was.

He took her in his arms, and she sighed against him. Where she was meant to be.

"I love you, Sadie."

"You're just saying that because I can make jam."

"There's plenty of evidence that you can make a mess. The jam, I'm not so sure about."

With a light heart she produced her single jar of jam from the fridge. "Stick your finger in that."

He did. Laughter lit his eyes when he tasted it. "I'll be damned, Sadie McGee. All this and you make jam?"

"All this?"

"All this tenderness, all this bold heart, all this originality, all this that you are. And you can make jam."

"Better grab me while you can."

He sobered. "As a matter of fact, I have something for you to stick your finger in, too." He took a little square velvet wrapped box from his jean pocket.

She stared at it, and then at him. She licked her lips and wiped her hands on her jeans. With trembling hands, she took the box and opened it.

A beautiful ring winked at her—simple, small and delicate. If she had picked a ring herself, this is the one she would have picked.

She knew before she slid it on her finger it would fit her perfectly.

It did.

"Are you just trying that on for size," he asked her, "or can we make this official?"

"We can make it official," she whispered.

He came and stood before her. He took her hands in his. He looked deep into her eyes.

"Will you marry me, Sadie?"

The tears glittered in her eyes again.

She couldn't trust herself to speak.

"I love you," he told her. "I've loved you for a long, long time. My heart waited for you to come home. I need to know if you feel the same way I do."

She nodded.

"No. Say it."

So she forced the words past the tears. "I'll marry you. I'll love you forever. I'll have your children. I'll make jam. I'll paint fire trucks. I'll knock out walls at the fire hall."

He was smiling. "You'll fly kites, and slide down fire poles, and teach little ones to ride bikes, and probably ponies, too. And, Sadie, you'll absolutely knock 'em dead down at the chamber of commerce. Sleepy Grove will probably become some sort of international destination."

She smiled at him through tears.

"All this love I'm going to give you, Sadie, is going to be like fuel inside you. Today, you'll take on Sleepy Grove—"

"Show me."

In answer he reached for her and wrapped his arms around her.

In answer his lips touched her forehead and her ears and her neck.

In answer he took her lips with his.

"Bring on the world," she whispered against his lips.

Epilogue

The backyard of Sam and Mickey McGee's house was packed to overflowing. It seemed the whole town of Sleepy Grove was there, from the mayor to the entire volunteer fire department.

The bride, radiant in yards and yards of white silk, arrived in a bright red antique fire truck. Her only jewelry was a small, gold St. Christopher's medallion. She walked slowly down the aisle formed by row after row of wooden chairs borrowed from the town hall.

The groom waited for her under the bright spring leaves of a giant maple tree, splendidly handsome in his pure black tux.

"He always was a handsome devil," Wenda murmured to her escort, Kevin. "But today he's fabulous. Look at the light in his eyes. Look at that little smile."

"I've already lost one woman to him," Kevin said with mock sternness. "Keep your eyes on me."

Wenda giggled.

Mickey McGee, the bride's brother stood on the groom's

right, looking handsome and carefree, with his long hair and formal dress. To Mickey's right was a little old man with cotton candy hair and twinkly blue eyes.

Walking slowly behind the bride, her hands clasping a basket full to overflowing with wildflowers, came Samantha McGee.

A little sigh went up from the crowd.

She looked beautiful. Every bit as beautiful as the bride. Radiant, healthy, alive.

Kate Adams came next, and whispers were exchanged that Kate had predicted this union a long time ago.

Behind Kate, came her son, handsome but sending dark and glowering looks at the little girl who rode the shaggy brown-and-white pony he was leading.

Amber sat regally sidesaddle, her face lit from within with happiness, a basket with the ring in it on her lap.

Kate's astonishing gifts were not needed to predict the future for those two.

"If you eat that ring today, Pom-Pom Angelo," Amber told her friend in a bossy no-nonsense voice, "no apples for a whole month."

Tucker, clutching his handmade fire truck, sat squirming in his seat between two sets of grandparents. Tyler snored against his grandpa Height's shoulder.

The bride reached the groom.

She looked at him for a long, long time. He looked back at her, unblinking. What they felt for one another danced softly in the air between them. Wonder. Love. Passion. Respect.

The minister had to clear his throat to get their attention.

Their hands touched, twined.

They turned to the minister to speak the words, to give the vows that their hearts had already spoken and given.

Angelo, the pig-eyed pony, reached around and helped

himself to a large mouthful of flowers from the maid of honor's basket.

With his mouth dripping stems and blossoms, he swung his head back to the laughing crowd.

And anybody who knew anything at all about angels would have sworn that he winked.

*   *   *   *   *

Share in the joy of yuletide romance with brand-new
stories by two of the genre's most beloved writers

DIANA PALMER

and

JOAN JOHNSTON

in

LONE STAR CHRISTMAS

Diana Palmer and Joan Johnston share their favorite
Christmas anecdotes and personal stories in this
special hardbound edition.

Diana Palmer delivers an irresistible spin-off of her
LONG, TALL TEXANS series and Joan Johnston crafts an
unforgettable new chapter to **HAWK'S WAY** in this wonderful
keepsake edition celebrating the holiday season. So
perfect for gift giving, you'll want one for yourself...and
one to give to a special friend!

Available in November at your favorite retail outlet!

Only from

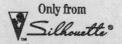
Silhouette®

Look us up on-line at: http://www.romance.net   JJDPXMAS

Take 4 bestselling love stories FREE

Plus get a FREE surprise gift!

Special Limited-time Offer

Mail to Silhouette Reader Service™

3010 Walden Avenue
P.O. Box 1867
Buffalo, N.Y. 14240-1867

YES! Please send me 4 free Silhouette Romance™ novels and my free surprise gift. Then send me 6 brand-new novels every month, which I will receive months before they appear in bookstores. Bill me at the low price of $2.67 each plus 25¢ delivery and applicable sales tax, if any.* That's the complete price and a savings of over 10% off the cover prices—quite a bargain! I understand that accepting the books and gift places me under no obligation ever to buy any books. I can always return a shipment and cancel at any time. Even if I never buy another book from Silhouette, the 4 free books and the surprise gift are mine to keep forever.

215 BPA A3UT

Name	(PLEASE PRINT)
Address	Apt. No.
City	State	Zip

This offer is limited to one order per household and not valid to present Silhouette Romance™ subscribers. *Terms and prices are subject to change without notice. Sales tax applicable in N.Y.

USROM-696   ©1990 Harlequin Enterprises Limited

You've been waiting for him all your life....
Now your Prince has finally arrived!

In fact, *three* handsome princes
are coming your way in

ROYAL WEDDINGS

A delightful new miniseries by **LISA KAYE LAUREL**
about three bachelor princes who find happily-ever-
after with three small-town women!

Coming in September 1997—THE PRINCE'S BRIDE

Crown Prince Erik Anders would do anything for his
country—even plan a pretend marriage to his lovely
castle caretaker. But could he convince the king, and
the rest of the world, that his proposal was real—before
his cool heart melted for his small-town "bride"?

Coming in November 1997—THE PRINCE'S BABY

Irresistible Prince Whit Anders was shocked to
discover that the summer romance he'd had years
ago had resulted in a very royal baby! Now that
pretty Drew Davis's secret was out, could her kiss
turn the sexy prince into a full-time dad?

**Look for prince number three in the exciting
conclusion to ROYAL WEDDINGS,
coming in 1998—only from**

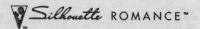

Silhouette ROMANCE™

Wanted: Brides! This small South Dakota town
needs women of marriageable age. And
Silhouette Romance invites you to visit the
handsome, extremely eligible men of:

a new miniseries by
Sandra Steffen

♥ The local veterinarian finds himself falling for his feisty
receptionist—the one woman in town *not* interested in
finding herself a husband.

LUKE'S WOULD-BE BRIDE
(June '97)

♥ This sheriff's got a reputation for being the good guy, yet a
certain single gal has him wanting to prove just what a wolf in
sheep's clothing he really is.

WYATT'S MOST WANTED WIFE
(August '97)

♥ A rugged rancher proposes a marriage of convenience to a
dowdy diner waitress, but just wait till his ugly-duckling
bride turns into a swan.

CLAYTON'S MADE-OVER MRS.
(October '97)

Don't miss any of these wonderful love stories, available only from

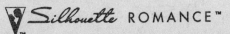

Bestselling author

JOAN JOHNSTON

continues her wildly popular miniseries with an
all-new, longer-length novel

The Virgin Groom

HAWK'S WAY

One minute, Mac Macready was a living legend in
Texas—every kid's idol, every man's envy, every
woman's fantasy. The next, his fiancée dumped him,
his career was hanging in the balance and his future
was looking mighty uncertain. Then there was the
matter of his scandalous secret, which didn't stand a
chance of staying a secret. So would he succumb to
Jewel Whitelaw's shocking proposal—or take cold
showers for the rest of the long, hot summer...?

Available August 1997
wherever Silhouette books are sold.

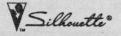

Silhouette®

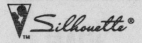